LIGHT AND TENDER BLUE

and Other Stories from the Sixties

By

Paul David Robinson

Cover design by Katrina Joyner

Copyright 1960-64, 2018

Kindle Direct Publishing Edition

LIGHT AND TENDER BLUE

and Other Stories from the Sixties

By

Paul David Robinson

Cover design by Katrina Joyner

Copyright 1960-64, 2018

Kindle Direct Publishing Edition

ISBN-13: 978-1-944675-17-2

ISBN-10: 1-944675-17-5

LIGHT AND TENDER BLUE
and Other Stories from the Sixties

TABLE OF CONTENTS

TITLE	PAGE
LIGHT AND TENDER BLUE	4
AMOEBOID	15
THE ANIMAL HOSPITAL	25
GOING HOME	32
ENIGMA FOR EMPIRICISTS	51
WITH MY HANDS	57
WHY IS THERE A RAINBOW?	72
MOVIN' IN	79
COME PLAY WITH ME	102
FINAL DECISION	122
PANACEA	153
MOMENT'S ILLUSION	166
Postscript	172
MARK OF THE BEAST Part one	174
MARK OF THE BEAST Part two	202
SECOND EARTH	212
Dear Reader	242

LIGHT AND TENDER BLUE

"Morning! Waking time!" my body kept telling my mind, but still it refused to be aroused. I rolled over and hit my head on a hard surface. I blinked and reached for the covers to pull them over my head.

No Covers! They must have fallen to the floor.

I rolled to the edge of the bed and reached over the side. My hand touched a hard surface level with my bed. I pulled my hand toward me caressing the surface, searching for the edge of my bed.

There was no edge!

I rose to my hands and knees with a start, wide awake. Had I fallen out of bed in the middle of the night and not been conscious of the fact?

I ran my hand over the floor absent-mindedly.

It was smooth and warm, having no cracks such as a wood or tile floor would have.

Warm!

I came out of my trance.

It was winter outside!

I ran my hand over the surface again, giving my action complete attention.

The surface was smooth and warm and there was a faint bluish glow around my hand. I lifted my hand from the surface and the glow disappeared.

I put my hand down again. On its contact with the floor, the bluish glow was there again. I moved my hand along the surface of the floor and the glow followed, affecting only the immediate surface around my hand.

I looked at the surface beneath my other hand: the glow was there. I looked to where my knees and feet touched the surface: the glow was there. I stood up and the only glow discernable was beneath my feet. All the rest of the floor or surface was dark; lighter than black, but dark.

I looked up and saw an endless translucent blue like the sky on a cloudless summer's day. There was no sun, no visible point-source of light. The blue hovered above me and the floor, touching the dark surface only in the distant horizon that was all around me.

I looked down at myself and for the first time I noticed that I was naked. I looked up at the sky (Was it a sky?) and then squatted down to compare the bluish glow of the floor beneath my feet with the lustrous blue of the sky.

Both blues were alike: a light and tender blue. The sky was just a shade deeper in color and I attributed that to its greater depth.

I sat down to think.

Was I awake?

I tried to open my eyes to find myself awakened from a dream and staring up at the night-darkened ceiling of my dormitory room.

It was no use. After a mental effort that gave me a headache, I decided that I really was awake and not dreaming.

I sighed. The sigh sounded like the

March Lion blowing through the trees, over grass, and against a loose windowpane – all in one. It was like an echoing sound in an enclosed and almost empty room.

The thought came to me that I was an experimental animal in a laboratory environment with my observers on the other side of one-way windows.

Trembling, I stood up; ashamed of my nakedness but indignant that they should have put me in such a predicament.

I looked around for an object to throw and end my anxiety with the shattering of glass. There was nothing to see on the surface around me.

I sighed again, but not so loudly as before.

Turning my head and body without moving my feet, I searched the horizon for some outstanding point by which to orient myself: I was standing on a center point encircled by a far and distant, smooth and level horizon.

I sighed with an inaudible, inward sigh and began to walk in the direction my feet were pointing.

Am I alone? I thought.

I raised my head and opened my mouth to shout, but whatever sound I would have made died in my throat.

I stopped walking just as I had taken another step and froze in position, keeping my mouth open for several moments. Finally, I closed my mouth and lowered my head. From there the motion was continuous. I seemed to melt slowly, ending on my hands and knees with my forehead pressed against the surface beneath me and my eyes closed in prayer.

"My God!" I whispered to the floor. "Where am I: in heaven; in hell?"

The hysterical quality in my voice shocked me. I put my elbows on the floor, clasped my hands behind my head against the base of my skull. I rested there with the top of my head pressed against the floor.

After a minute or two of incoherent thought, I began to speak aloud to myself: "I am not really lonely. I'm just not with people! What do I care if I wear no clothes? It was society that insisted that I do so!"

I leaned backwards until I rested on the floor with my legs straight out before me and my hands behind my head. I looked up at the placid blue sky.

I said aloud, "No birds! No grass! No trees! I guess one doesn't even miss those when there are no people."

I stretched my hands above my head, closed my eyes, and tensed every muscle in my body. Then I relaxed and brought my hands back beneath my head again. I looked up into the sky, took a deep breath, and closed my eyes.

"Oh, God," I breathed, "maybe I should be anxious and afraid yet, but I'm not."

After a moment I asked, "Do you think I should want to share this moment of peace with someone else? I do feel some emptiness, a lack of fulfillment – but I don't want someone to talk with. I just want someone who could share this moment with me; someone to feel the peace that I feel.

"We'd just lay – she and I – side by

side feeling your presence within us and knowing heaven: the eternal peace of love and beauty found in the silence of a moment.

"I don't know why I should think it necessary for my companion to be female unless it is because of my conditioning; the result of being born a member of a heterosexual society."

I sat up and looked around. I was on a hill now, surrounded by an immense field of grass. A gentle wind was blowing; and there was a sun and a few white, billowy clouds in the sky.

My breath caught in the shock. Slowly I looked down at myself. I was still naked! I relaxed in relief.

I lay back and looked up at the sky through a screen of slender blades of grass. A seed-stem bent down beneath the weight of its progeny and tickled my nose until I had to brush it away.

Above me a sheep-cloud gamboled across the sky accompanied by a much more streamlined antelope cloud.

I rolled over onto my stomach and buried my face in the pillow of grass. I could smell the sweet scent of the earth beneath the grass. I placed my cheek against the sod and closed my hands into fists and held onto the grass that touched my hands. I was holding myself tight to the ground as though I would float away if I didn't.

I heard the sound of a lark and I raised my head and strained my ears toward the sound. Then I saw its drab body flittering here and there. I sat up and watched it. It drew near me after several of its short flights and I could plainly hear its song. Then another lark flew near and I heard a short duet before both birds flew away.

I decided to follow them since I had nothing else to do. I walked down the hill and nearly stepped on a dandelion. I didn't pick it. Instead, I bent down to smell it. It didn't have a pleasant odor like a rose, but it was a pretty flower. I touched it gently and brushed my cheek against it. It was soft and cool.

I looked around for companion flowers and saw none. I was doubly grateful that I noticed that bit of gold in a field of grass before I stepped on it.

I climbed another rise of land and saw a tree in the distance. It was on another hill and silhouetted against the sky.

I walked down into the shallow valley and up the hill where the tree stood. It was a beautiful tree. It was a birch tree with a white trunk and branches spotted with brown. It had dainty green leaves for trimming.

When I stood beneath it, I looked up to its uppermost branches. It seemed to be reaching for the sky. The tree seemed to have personal contact with and an affinity for the outermost regions of the universe.

I was gazing up in admiration for the tree with sun shining full on my face one moment and the next instant I was standing on a crowded sidewalk with sun on my face and looking up at a beautiful skyscraper towering above me.

When I realized another transition had taken place, I looked around. I was surrounded by people. The people were laughing and pointing at me. I looked down at myself. I was naked.

I searched the crowd for a friendly face. Many of my acquaintances were part of this leering mob. I looked beyond them and saw a young woman off by her self. Her eyes met mine. They held a look of understanding and empathy as though she also knew the hardships of deviating from the norm.

I began to walk toward her and into the crowd. The crowd broke as I moved forward, leaving a pathway open.

I hadn't gone but a few steps when someone shouted: "Don't let him come among us! He's different! He's abnormal!"

Immediately the parted mass pressed together and thrust me away from them and back into the center of the surrounding crowd. I had nowhere to go. I had to stand there and wait for whatever happened next.

I looked beyond the crowd at the young woman off by herself. Her face was full of sadness. Slowly she turned and walked away and I had not the strength or courage to follow her.

I knew I was home. [1]

---

[1] This was written in the fall of 1963. I lived in Union City, Ohio at the time.

AMOEBOID

Sometimes the crowds watching the ore boats at Sault Saint Marie are pulsing like gargantuan amoeba. One individual as part of the living organism cannot help but move when the crowd moves. An amoeba moves slowly; so will the crowd. The crowd often freezes motionless; as does the amoeba. Unless people are tied together by bonds stronger than affection or are exceptionally rude, they will be separated by the slow pulsations of the crowd.

One moment a young man will be standing with a comrade; shortly, that same young man is vainly searching for his fellow: He has been separated almost surreptitiously from his comrade by – well, he could never tell how many people.

There is very little chance that the same two people would be thrust together again after they had once been separated by the organism's motion. After they are separated, the surest way for two people to find one another again would be for each to leave the crowd and search for one another in the immensity of the emptiness without the whole.

Society is like that. When friends or lovers are separated by the whirls of movement within the pulsating mass, they must leave society behind, turn their backs on the protection found in numbers, and face a great unknown, if they would find identity with one another once more.

While a part of a particular crowd at Sault Saint Marie, Donald Farelane was separated from his traveling companions. Donald first found himself surrounded by people and a view of the locks lost to him. Three minutes of patiently waiting for the organism to writhe and turn into itself again and Donald stood before the rail and was looking down at the locks.

The water was receding, lowering

the ore boat to the level of Lake Huron. It was only a few seconds before Donald was aware of the young woman standing beside him. She had orange-red hair. Her skin was unblemished and untanned. She wore shorts and a blouse. There was a pair of binoculars hanging by its cord around her neck and lying against her breasts.

As Donald looked at her, he became aware of the feeling of her. Her body and mind seemed to emanate her emotional state. Donald recalled reading a book once that referred to one of the female characters as a "bitch in heat." If this pretty woman had not the same inner turmoil as that woman in the book, Donald would have cut his own throat; he was that certain of his instinct. He looked at the young woman's figure with aroused, avid interest.

When there was a slight movement within the crowd, Donald was able to direct his own motion toward the young woman. She was one of the few who did not move at all during that pulsation.

Donald was more and more aware

of her proximity. His thigh pressed against the back of her hip. He could feel the tension within her body increasing; without looking, the young woman knew it was a man who was so close to her. Slowly she turned her head to look at Donald's face.

She saw a clean-shaven young man with light brown hair and blue-green eyes. He wore corrective lenses, but his jaw was firm and his face smooth and tanned; his body was lithe and strong. And Donald saw the finest nose and mouth combination he had ever noticed on a woman. Her eyebrows were dark and thin and her eyes were green, true green.

The young woman quickly turned her head and looked down at the ore boat. Donald was acutely aware of her now; he moved his leg and his shin was against the calf of her leg. The people around them moved and the young man and young woman were pushed closer to the rail and closer together.

The young woman took up her binoculars and raised them to her eyes.

As she looked out at Lake Superior, her shoulder pressed against Donald's chest. He could feel her breathe and he knew that she could feel him breathe. His exhalation brushed against the back of her neck.

She stood motionless for a long while. Donald could feel the warmth of her body through her clothes and his clothes, from his shin touching her calf all the way up to her shoulder against his chest. He could feel the softness of her long, orange-red hair blowing gently against his neck and face. Her ear was so near he could have bent his head forward only an inch and his lips would touch its dainty lobe in a kiss. The desire to do just that was agony as he touched her waist with his fingertips.

His fingers felt her skin beneath the cloth. He could feel her catch her breath and hold it the moment that he touched her. His fingertips caressed her gently as she held her breath. Donald discovered that he was holding his breath with her.

She lay the binoculars down against her well formed breasts and leaned forward. While he leaned forward with her, Donald could feel her exhale in a silent shuddered sigh. She caught the top rail with both hands, her head bowed down.

With a shock, Donald found that his whole hand was held against her pliable side. He trembled as he slowly moved his hand from her warm abdomen and placed it on the rail beside one of hers.

Donald half-heartedly attempted to remain immobile, but his free hand just naturally moved from his side to her other hip; and from there, he could not keep it from moving up her back in a long caress. He felt the bumps of her spinal cord and the strap of her brassiere. He could feel the increased rapidity of her breathing. She raised her head and pressed her body tighter against his. Her cheek nearly touched his cheek.

They reached the breaking point together: That point in physical desire when a man and a woman either continue until the ultimate union is completed or discontinue their physical contact with one another and painfully await the cooling of their heated minds and bodies.

There were people around; they were strangers to one another; this was atop a tourist platform overlooking the locks of Sault Saint Marie; this was not a society that condoned the public display of lust; they were members of a mass that gave lip service to the sinfulness of lust without love, although there was much of the same lust without love in the privacy of bedrooms of married and unmarried couples; the two young people were afraid that to do what they desired to do at the moment would be wrong; they did not know each others' names, only the pleasure found in touching one another!

Donald and the young woman pulled apart as much as they could. They dared not even look at each other: their lust was so great. They stood silently without touching each other. Both were breathing deeply and rapidly and trying very hard to hide their emotional condition from those people around them. They attempted to force their minds away from the fact of their proximity and concentrate on the ore boat leaving the lock.

It would be difficult to say what Donald Farelane and this unknown woman would have done. Would they have finally left the crowd hand in hand to look for some close-at-hand secluded spot? Would they have just stood there with that agonizing desire within their yearning bodies and never speak a word to one another? Would they have finally left each other with just a parting glance after their heated bodies were cooled and under careful control?

There is no way of knowing what those two young people would have done for the decision was taken out of their hands. The amoeba writhed once more and the couple was separated forever without ever speaking or that backward glance.

When they searched for one another among the people of the crowd, they did not see one another. Both made their ways to the edge of the organism, but could not break from their ties with the crowd. They tried many times, yet each time, a greater fear of what they might find without the shelter of the mass kept them from discovering each other again.

When this particular crowd at the locks of Sault Saint Marie left this location en masse to rejoin the greater society, the two young people did not see one another; and each went a separate way.

Donald walked to the automobile where he would meet his traveling companions. He wondered, as he awaited his comrades, whether there was any truth in the many tales of love at first sight that he had read and heard about.

He knew that he had been greatly stirred by that pretty young woman with the green eyes and orange-red hair, but could such lust eventually become love? He did not know. He would never know.

He would think about this incident and wonder what the results would have been had he done this or that. He would always wonder about this recent incident and other past and future incidents as he was shoved here and there in the writhing of the greater amoeba.

He would search for someone many times to cling to and tie himself to so he would not be alone in his unpredictable and uncontrolled drifting within the bowels of the greater amoeba.

He might one day step out into the less crowded area surrounding the amoeba and truly find himself with some other without the inhibitions and aimlessness of the amoeba proper: outside, in the free universe; but he doubted that he would.[2]

---

[2] I wrote this in the summer of 1962 after a visit to Sault Saint Marie.

THE ANIMAL HOSPITAL

I was sure my pet was sick – he wasn't himself! Usually he would bounce around with matchless energy. Why only yesterday – I am sure it was just to be ornery, although he claimed it was on impulse – my pet climbed a tree. He went all the way to the topmost branch. It made me dizzy watching him sway back and forth, back and forth. I tried to coax him down: "Come on down, fella," I begged, "you're making me dizzy!"

He laughed at me and pulled himself higher up on the limb. He called, "It's nice up here. Come on up and join me." His voice showed his elation.

It made me furious that he did as he pleased. I called him every dirty name I could think of, but he just laughed and move out even farther.

I debated on going after him, but I was afraid. I figured that it would be best if I did not enter his element – if one of us did not stay on solid, sure ground, we both would suffer.

He whispered to me, "It's great up here! So clean and fresh! So beautiful!"

I just sat down on a nearby rock and waited for him to tire and come down.

He didn't tire. Four hours later, I was still waiting. Each minute my body temperature had gone up another degree. I was seething mad by that time. I shook the tree.

He laughed at me for a moment, and then he got seasick and ordered me to stop. I disregarded his pleasure – it was my revenge for his lack of consideration.

I shook the tree for ten minutes trying to unseat the darned pet, but he was too sure-footed. I quit shaking the tree and ordered him to come down. Sure that he had the upper hand, he spat in my face. He thought I would go after him, but I didn't. I left him there and returned shortly with an ax.

Amused, he watched the proceedings below him; he didn't believe

I would really undermine him until he felt the tree shudder in its final resistance.

I looked up, planning to smile in his face as he went down.

He pitied me with his eyes.

Then I knew I couldn't watch his destruction. I spread my arms and, as the tree began to fall, told him to jump. The force of his impact took us both to the ground.

He was the first to stand. He helped me up. I looked into his eyes with a puzzled expression. He turned away from me. He seemed to be disappointed.

The next morning, he sulked, curled up in out-of-the-way corners, hiding in the closet, or glaring at me from the opposite side of a convenient chair. In addition, he was a paragon of cooperation, obeying me implicitly – so much out of character! I was so worried that I took him to the family doctor.

I stayed with my pet as he was examined, answering questions about the possible causes of his malaise. After the preliminary examination, the doctor suggested my pet be admitted to the hospital for thorough physical and psychological examinations.

This worried me even more about my friend's state of health. I asked for a private session with the doctor since my pet could understand people all too well. The doctor led me to an adjoining room.

When alone with him, I asked, "Is it serious, Doctor?"

"Yes," he replied, "so serious that I think it wise that you stay with your friend at all times. He could be very troublesome without your presence."

"I can spare the time," I told the doctor.

That same day, my friend and I were given a room on the top floor of the hospital.

The several specialized personnel that came to observe my pet asked me all sorts of questions about him. I gave each of them his whole history. The doctors were fascinated that I could have such a pet and complimented me on him many times.

It pleased me very much. I had never thought of this friend as unusual; he had been with me all of my life – well, almost.

My pet found me one day while I was watching a sunset. I was admiring its beauty when all of a sudden this fellow appeared beside me. He asked what I was observing; I told him. He asked me how I thought of it. That puzzled me.

"How should I know?" I had bellowed, "I really don't care how I think of it!"

"Don't push the panic button," he had comforted, "I'll explain it to you."

I had only glared at him.

"All right! All right!" he had said, "I won't bother!"

I had ignored him the rest of the time, but he wouldn't go away. I refused to acknowledge his presence. When he coughed and fidgeted, he disturbed me, but I wasn't going to let him know it.

When I went home, he followed me. I had finally taken him in and we had become friendly adversaries: fond of each other, in a way.

My pet and I were at the hospital for several weeks. Eventually I was told that my pet was near death and would I please agree to stay with him when they transferred him to a new hospital.

Again, I was reluctant. I was worried about the amount of time I was spending. I was warned that the crisis would occur within the week. Understanding the gravity of the situation, I agreed.

When the doctors left, my pet said, "I'm tired of staying here. I am going to leave."

"But," I objected, "You're very seriously ill!"

He smiled wanly and said, "I'm not the one they think ill."

The realization exploded in my mind with the force of an atomic bomb. I dropped the novel I had been studying, jumped off the bed and ran to the door. It was locked!

I ran to the windows and tried them all. They were solid.

I turned in horror and watched as my embodied Id re-entered the realm of intangibles: He dissolved into the air![3]

---

[3] I wrote this for fun sometime while at Otterbein College. Except for summers, I was there from August 1963 – January, 1967. I would guess 1965. That's when I wrote a lot of these short stories.

GOING HOME

She was in the Columbus bus station waiting for the next bus to Cleveland. A pretty girl, seemingly much too young to be the mother of an eight-year-old boy! Her eyes were sad; mournful as a dog's when its young master had been gone from it too long. But there was a smile on her face, a smile for her child.

The boy was taking big bites from a twenty-five-cent hamburger (One could see it would not last long.) and taking big drags at a ten-cent coke. He was talking excitedly to his mother about Cleveland. He knew nothing about Cleveland, but he was energetically visualizing it as a Chicago, a New York City, and a Hollywood all rolled into one.

The boy's mother was only half-listening to her son's chatter. She was staring down into her glass of ice-water with the faraway look of a philosopher on her face. Every once in a while, a question asked by the boy would break through and she would smile at him and give him an answer that did not live up to his expectations of Cleveland. The boy was oblivious to his mother's thoughtfulness. He was at that age when every day is an adventure. Very little could have dulled his exuberance.

As her son took another bite of hamburger, the girl was left a few moments' peace. She looked down at her glass of water and ran her finger along the moisture that had collected on the outside. "Oh, why, why," she asked herself, "didn't Phil have insurance?" A tear glistened in the corner of one eye and slipped down to the end of her nose. She wiped it away with a small fist. She remembered the man who had come to the door of the small house they had rented.

"Mrs. Renni?" he'd said.

"Yes," she'd answered.

The man had shown her a badge and said, "Lieutenant Jennings, plainclothesman, ma'am."

"Yes, what can I do for you?" the

young housewife had asked.

"Ma'am, your husband was killed in a traffic accident at 2:30 this afternoon."
. . .

"Mom!" the boy interrupted. The mother turned to her son with a smile.

"Yes, Jimmy?" she asked.

"How much farther is it to Cleveland?"

"One hundred and forty miles," she answered softly.

"Gee!" exclaimed the boy, "I asked that once before, didn't I, Mom?" the boy asked incredulously.

The girl dimpled and said, "Yes, Jimmy." She bent down and kissed her son on the cheek.

"Aw, Mom!" he complained, "There's people watchin'." And he took another bite of hamburger to hide his embarrassment.

The young mother smiled at her son and then turned back to contemplate over the ice melting in her glass of water.

She smiled now as she remembered meeting Philip those nine years ago.

He'd been a sophomore in high school and she a lowly freshman when he'd come up to her during the high school dance.

"Hello," he'd said.

"Hi," she had answered shyly, "aren't you on the varsity basketball team?"

He had blushed. "Will you dance with me?" he'd asked.

She nodded and slipped within his arms for the slow dance.

"My name is Philip Renni."

"I am Dorothy Kaufman."

He was a terrible dancer, but she had managed. When it was over and a faster dance was coming up, he had been uncertain whether to chance asking her to dance again. Finally he had said, "Care for a coke?"

"I'd love to have one," Dorothy had answered.

A month later, they had exchanged rings. A year later, she left home to go with him when he ran away in his '49 Plymouth.

Philip Renni took his sixteen-year-old sweetheart to Tampa. There, they lied about their ages and were married in the chapel of a small Methodist church. The two kids worked at a motel restaurant as waitress and dishwasher until Dorothy was four months pregnant. Then, Philip packed his young wife and their few belongings in his old car and went to Texas. In Galveston, Philip found a job working in construction. Jimmy was soon to enter grade school before Philip realized that he wasn't gaining on his debts. He looked around for a better job and found one driving a truck for one of the lesser mining companies in Arizona. Two years later, he was dead; killed in a car-truck accident.

When all the debts were paid, there was nothing left. Neighbors chipped in for the bus fare to send Dorothy and her eight-year-old son home to her parents; Philip had no family.

Philip had been an illegitimate child living with some non-relation that had taken him in. He left no one to worry about his whereabouts when he ran away.

Dorothy's parents were in the lower middle class. Her father owned a small neighborhood grocery store.

When she left home, she did not write or leave a message. In eight years, she had never sent as much as a postcard or Christmas card home. An only child, she knew that if she had written during the first few months, she would have been brought home. After Jimmy was born, she hadn't cared to write home at all. But now, she needed someone.

"What will Dad and Mom say?" she thought. Her lower lip trembled and she gripped the counter for support. "Oh, I have been so unkind," she said to herself; and two big tears fell from each eye. "They have every right to say, 'Dorothy Kaufman? Never heard of her!'" she affirmed to herself. "But I have no other place to go!" . . .

"Mom?" asked the little boy.

"Yes, Jimmy?" she said softly, giving him her brave smile.

He leaned up and whispered in her

ear, "Where's the bathroom, Mom?"

The young mother whispered back, "It's up the stairs."

When her son was gone, Dorothy picked up her glass with both shaking hands and drank all of the water – there was no ice; it had all melted. She set the glass down and, taking a quick, deep breath that she released in a kind of sob, she stood up to her full five foot and one inch height. She felt only a little better inside: more resolute, but no less apprehensive.

She left the diner and sat down on a bench below the stairs to await her son. She looked at the other passengers waiting for their buses.

How many, she wondered, were going to Cleveland?

She didn't wonder for long, because the word "Cleveland" made her thoughtful again.

She invented conversations in her mind – conversations she might have with her parents. Some were nasty and troubled her; others were pleasant, but still troubled her. She could not imagine her parents forgiving her for eight years of neglect.

"Bus for Cleveland: Gate A - Lane three; Departure in fifteen minutes!" came the metallic voice over the loudspeaker.

Dorothy looked around for her son. She saw him at the newsstand reading a comic book. Dorothy walked over to where she had left their suitcase and moved it to the end of the bench nearest the newsstand. She then came up behind Jimmy and looked over his shoulder: He was reading an ACTION comic that featured Superman.

Jimmy became aware of someone standing behind him and looked back over his shoulder. "Hi, Mom," he said to his girlish mother, "is it time to go?"

"Yes, Jimmy."

The boy closed the comic book and put it back where it belonged. Dorothy was proud that he had not asked to keep it. She led the way back to their suitcase.

"How long will it take, Mom?" Jimmy asked.

Dorothy picked up the suitcase by its handle and looked for the way to lane three. "About four hours, Jimmy," she answered. She saw the sign: Gate A – lanes 1, 2, & 3. She walked toward that door.

"It's six now, Mom. We won't get there until ten o'clock," Jimmy observed.

The young mother made no comment.

They stood in a line for a long time before they finally came to the driver taking the tickets.

"Two for Cleveland?" the driver asked.

"Yes," said Dorothy.

"Shall I put your suitcase with the luggage underneath?" he asked. "You won't be trading buses again."

"No thank you," Dorothy answered. "We will be getting off before we get to the bus station."

"All right," said the driver. "Here, let me take the suitcase. I'll put it on the luggage rack above your seat for you."

"Thank you very much."

Dorothy and Jimmy sat together two seats behind the driver. In an hour, they were both asleep. Dorothy awoke when the bus made a short stopover in Ashland. She did not wake Jimmy, but left the bus for a drink of water. Jimmy was still sleeping when she returned.

As the bus left Ashland and continued on its way toward Cleveland, Dorothy recalled her dream. She had dreamed that her parents had died in her absence and she would never see them again. She thought of her childhood and those incidents that she could never forget. She smiled to herself as she recalled the many things she had done with her parents.

It began to rain.

She remembered a certain Sunday when she and her parents were to have gone on a picnic, but it had rained. The three of them stayed home and had the picnic anyway. Her mother had spread a tablecloth on the green rug in the living room. They hadn't cooked any hotdogs, but each had made his own cold chicken and cold bologna sandwiches there in the living room. That was sixteen years ago.

Dorothy began to cry softly to herself. In his sleep, Jimmy moved closer to his mother and she clasped him to her bosom.

The rain had stopped half an hour before. Jimmy was awake now and, by the light of the full moon, Dorothy was pointing out to him the different places she remembered from her childhood. They were nearing the suburb of Cleveland where she had lived.

Most of this section of Cleveland had changed so much in the last eight years that Dorothy was hard pressed to find places she found familiar. She was coming closer to the block where her father had his grocery store. She was full of expectation. When the bus slowed down to let her off at the address she had given the driver, she saw a large shopping center instead of the familiar storefront grocery store of her memory.

Dorothy was shocked, but she couldn't let Jimmy know that she was lost. The driver took her suitcase down from the luggage rack and set it on the sidewalk for her as she and Jimmy followed him off of the bus.

The bus driver looked around him and then down at the young woman. "Don't you think it would be better if you came down to the bus depot?" the driver asked politely.

Dorothy smiled bravely and said, "We'll be all right, thank you."

The driver touched his cap and was gone.

Dorothy and Jimmy watched the bus until it was out of sight.

"Where do we go from here?" Jimmy asked.

Dorothy looked around. In the street lights, she saw the name of the large supermarket in the shopping center: KAUFMAN'S SUPERMARKET! She looked for a telephone booth and soon saw one a block away. She Picked up the suitcase and took Jimmy's hand.

When they came to the telephone booth, Dorothy left Jimmy to sit on the suitcase and she entered the booth. She closed the door and opened the telephone book.   She looked for the entry: Kaufman, Allen J. She found the name and marked it with her fingernail. Then, knowing before hand that it was no use, she searched her pockets and purse for a dime.   She shrugged her shoulders when she found none.

She looked at her parents' new address and memorized it.   Then she looked for its location on the map of Cleveland and its suburbs that appeared in the telephone book. In relation to where she was now, her parents' house was a distance of twenty city-blocks. Dorothy sighed.

She left the booth and found her son dozing. While sitting down on the suitcase, he was leaning to one side with his elbows on the suitcase and his head on his hands. Dorothy bent down and kissed his neck. Jimmy was instantly awake. He sat up and smiled sheepishly for no reason at all.

"What do we do now, Mom?" the boy asked.

She answered, "We're going for a long walk."

She picked up the suitcase, took Jimmy's hand, and started back the way they had come.

After they had walked two blocks, Dorothy said to her little boy, "Shall I tell you a story about another Jimmy and his Rover Bear?"

Enthusiastically, Jimmy said, "Sure, Mom!"

Dorothy told him an imaginative tale about a boy who looked very much like her son Jimmy and who had a magical teddy bear he called Rover Bear. Rover Bear was always taking his master on trips to different places all over the world when his master should have been sleeping. The comradely pair would take trips to Easter Island where egg-laying bunnies were, or to the Arabian Desert in search of the Phoenix bird, or to the South Pole to visit the city of Triton that existed beneath all the ice and snow. These trips would last until the wee hours of the morning. Just before time to wake up, Rover Bear and his master would hurry home in time for the little boy to wake up.

"It was a funny thing," said Dorothy as she finished the story, "but that other Jimmy would be tired everyday until he finally stopped dreaming that he had taken those trips with his teddy bear."

"Aw, Mom!" said Jimmy, "I don't believe that."

Dorothy laughed at him. They were only two or three blocks from her parents' house. The story had lasted for fifteen blocks.

"You don't really think something like that could happen, do you Mom?" Jimmy persisted.

"It might, Jimmy," she said, "but it happens most often in dreams."

"You're a great story-teller, Mom!" Jimmy said with pride.

Dorothy laughed again despite the growing uneasiness within her mind and body. She set their suitcase down and took Jimmy in her arms. She kissed him four times on the forehead. Jimmy didn't put up his usual struggle of protest this time, but let her fondle him.

Dorothy stopped and held him away from her so she could look at him: he looked so much like his father. She kissed him one more time, on the cheek.

"We haven't far to go now, Jimmy," she said. She took his hand, and then picked up the suitcase.

They were in a new section now; one that had just recently been built. All the houses were of the fifteen to twenty-five thousand dollar bracket.[4] They came to the house with the address Dorothy had memorized. It was a large, stone affair of the low, ranch-house style with a two-car garage. It was in the center of a large fenced-in yard.

Dorothy looked at the name on the mailbox: Mr. and Mrs. Allen J. Kaufman.

She looked again at the house she saw before her. It was so different from the two-story frame storefront house she remembered living in during her childhood. She was afraid to go up to the door.

Dorothy looked around her fearfully.

"Mom," Jimmy asked in a whisper, "is this it?"

Strengthened by her child's need,

---

[4] That was in 1964. That would be two hundred thousand or more in 2018.

Dorothy said slowly, "Yes, it is."

Dorothy took his hand and the suitcase and they walked up the driveway. She followed the sidewalk to the front door.   She set the suitcase down, away from the door, and whispered for Jimmy to stay with it.

She walked up to the front door. It had a screen door in front of it.   She caressed the doorframe next to the doorbell with the fingertips of her right hand. Then she circled the doorbell with one finger several times before she placed her finger on its pearly smoothness.   She took a deep breath and released is slowly. She stabbed the button once with her finger. She could hear chimes playing a short tune.

It seemed an eternity, but it was only about a minute before a light came on in the house and Dorothy heard footsteps coming toward the door. Tension was mounting within her as she waited. The footsteps drew nearer and nearer. The porch lights came on and Dorothy audibly gasped under their bright scrutiny. The door swung open into the house.

"Yes?" said a rather irritated masculine voice, "What may I do for you?"

The girl's heart was beating so fast and her breathing was so heavy that it was a full thirty seconds before she could say anything.

During those thirty seconds all the imaginary conversations she had planned came to her mind. She hastened to recall all of those first greetings she had experimented with. At last, she blurted out something she had never thought of using.

"Daddy?" she asked tremulously.

There was silence on the other side of the screen door. Slowly the screen door opened and the porch light flooded upon the robed figure of a yet athletic man of fifty-five. He stared down at his visitor – his tanned face tense beneath his snow-white, uncombed hair.

"Allen?" called a voice that Dorothy knew from a shadowed figure behind him, "Who is it at this time of night?"

Now, the left cheek of the man

trembled in a muscle spasm. His mouth came open as he took a step forward.

Dorothy stepped back and pulled Jimmy toward her. "Mom, Dad," she whispered uncertainly, "your grandson."

The man reached down with his strong arms and picked up the eight-year-old boy. He hugged the child to his chest.

"How are you, Sport?" Allen Kaufman asked his grandson.[5]

---

[5] I saw a mother with her child at the Columbus, Ohio bus station. The boy was eating a hamburger and the mother was counting out her change on the table beside the boy. It seemed to be the last of her money for their trip. I wrote this story on my bus ride back to Union City, Ohio where I lived at that time. That was 1963.

ENIGMA FOR EMPIRICISTS

Toni and Joan had often ridden the train together, but this was the first time they had ridden while sitting on opposite sides of the car. They hadn't originally planned to sit apart. Joan had suggested the novelty.

As the two girls entered the day-coach, Joan had remarked that they had always sat together, sharing the sights to be seen through one window. This was an opportune time, Joan had suggested, for them to sit on opposite sides of the train and watch for particularly interesting sights. The moment either of the girls would see something unusual, she was to call the other who would then cross the aisle to see as well.

This was a greater opportunity than either girl could have realized. On that day of all days, the machinery of the train had been malfunctioning. Due to circumstances beyond the machinery's control, there had been an uncommon drain of energy. The loss of this energy had prevented the illusionator from attaining minimum operating power. This resulted in the machinery's inability to sustain the necessary, identically time-sequenced illusions on both sides of the train track. The malfunction would not have been noticed had the two young ladies sat on the same side: either right or left; it would not have mattered. In either case, the machinery could have given them the expected illusion on the one side, and the girls might never have known the secret of the other side.

Since the two girls had sat on opposite sides of the train, their separation forced the illusionator to make a random choice of which side would receive the illusion. It just happened that Joan sat on the side where the illusion was sustained. Joan saw through her window the typical barnyards, ponds, corn fields, roads, telephone poles, houses and railroad crossings.

Toni sat staring in fascination through her window; she saw a flat, treeless, grassless, sand-smooth area surrounded by a huge ring of connected railroad cars. She saw that she was in one of the railroad cars encircling the sand-area as the ring of horses on a carousel would spin around the calliope and other machinery.

Toni called to Joan and Joan quickly crossed the aisle to join her. The moment Joan would look through Toni's window, the illusionator would abandon Joan's side and replace the odd scene with the counterpart of the illusion Joan had been seeing on her own side.

When Joan looked through the window, Toni was flabbergasted to see that the scene on her side had changed. Now Toni was seeing the ordinary view of a cow pasture slipping away along the side of the train. Nevertheless, Toni described for Joan what she had seen but a moment before.

Joan was puzzled as she returned to her own side. When she looked through her window, she was shocked to see the mirrored duplicate of what Toni had described for her. Joan called Toni over to her side.

The moment Toni could discern anything through Joan's window, she saw a little boy yelling and waving to the engineer. Although Joan was now seeing what Toni saw, she told her friend that until Toni joined her, she had seen the sand-area encircled by the ring of connected railroad cars.

Toni returned to her own side and saw the odd scene that she had seen before Joan joined her the first time. Toni told Joan that the sand-area and the circle of railroad cars were on her side again.

Joan and Toni experimented by switching sides and crossing and re-crossing the aisle. Finally, the girls were convinced that something was not right with their world. If the ring of connected railroad cars encircling the sand-area was a reality, how was it that the train could circle both to the left and to the right at the same instant?

The girls decided to go through the

railroad cars and walk to the end of the train – if there were an end. They left behind them the few belongings they had brought with them for the trip. After thirty minutes of walking, the girls re-entered the railroad car that held their belongings at the opposite end of it.

Toni and Joan were very confused and very frightened. Despite their fears and confusion, the two young ladies elected to walk in opposite directions. Toni sought to find the caboose; and Joan hoped to discover a diesel engine. The girls met each other when they re-entered their car from opposite ends without passing one another on their walks.

Almost terrified, the two girls sat together for company until the train made its stop at their destination. As each girl collected her belongings, she looked through the window she had when she started their journey.

Joan looked out on the bustle of the train station; Toni saw the sand-area encircled by the railroad cars – the railroad cars were at rest. The girls planned one more experiment: Each would leave by the exit on her own side of the train.

The girls never saw each other again. Joan stepped onto the train station platform; Toni stepped out onto the sand. Joan stepped back into life; Toni stepped into reality.[6]

---

[6] This was submitted May 11, 1965. It was intended to suggest that we may never know the meaning of life or anything else.

WITH MY HANDS

My name is Jennifer and I am going to tell you about something mysterious that happened to me this summer.

I'm not sure where he came from. He just walked in one day while Mom was baking bread. It was Saturday and Dad was painting the picket fence. I was pulling weeds in the flower beds and I heard him; he was kicking pebbles on the tar road as he walked. I looked up and he looked at me as he walked.

He had his hands in his pockets and he walked by the mailbox and stepped into the yard. He walked through the gateway and across the yard looking at me. Dad said later that he came so slowly that he didn't notice him walk up. I just know that he looked at me as he walked.

He stopped walking when he was about three feet from me. He stood there with his hands in the pockets of his jeans looking down at me and what I had been doing.

I was aware of the old jeans and stained shirt I was wearing, the rusty trowel in my hand, the dirt on my cheek and in my hair, and the pile of weeds between my knees.

He smiled and said:

> "A job
> you have been doing
> is what I should have
> to keep my interest from myself
> in thoughtful moving hands."

He knelt down beside me and took my hands and then the trowel from my hand. He looked at me, not at my dirty cheek, and smiled.

He said:

> "Your hand held this
> show me how
> to do with this?"

I didn't answer. I was watching his face. He was most intent.

He said:

> "The point for stabbing
> breaks the soil and makes
> crumbles for the flowers' roots
> as the wrist is twisting."

"Job, son?" Dad's low voice asked.

That startled me. I hadn't heard Dad's step.

He looked up at Dad and smiled. Then he faded the smile and his eyes were just intent.

He said:

"Yes."

He stood up and handed me the trowel without looking down

Dad asked, "Will you paint my fence?"

He said:

"I might as well paint
a picket fence with time
and my hands not busy now.
But why picket fence paint
white over white.
The color is light
but blue is soft
and aqua cool."

Dad said, "The fence has always been white. I paint it white because then it takes just one coat."

He said:

"Alternate blue with white

for matching house-trim, shutters, and fence."

Dad said, "Yes. There is blue in the garage. I'll show you." Dad smiled now.

Between pulling weeds, I watched him paint. He painted without stop, slowly, intently. He spattered not a drop on the grass or on his clothes. Dad watched him from the porch and from the garden when vegetables were picked for supper.

The fence was almost painted when I finished weeding and went inside to help Mom. Dad was watching out the kitchen window.

Dad said, "He paints slowly but he doesn't stop. I didn't expect him to finish today, but he will."

I asked, "Did he tell you his name, Daddy?"

Dad was surprised. "I was going to ask you that, Jennifer."

Mom was listening. Now she said, "He's a nice looking boy, whoever he is."

I said, "Yes, whoever he is."

Dad wondered, "Should we ask him

to stay for dinner?"

Mom said, "I had planned on a guest, Jim."

"Oh," said Dad, "I'll ask him to stay."

Mom took the meatloaf out of the oven.

The doorbell rang and I almost ran to the door and I would have if I hadn't remembered who was outside.

Dad was grinning at me and Mom was waiting.

I smiled sheepishly and went to my room.

Dad went to the door.

The boy was standing there.

Dad said, "Well, all done now, son?"

David said:

"Yes. Fence is blue now
and white.
I pattern painted posts
trimmed with white."

Dad said, "That's a beautiful paint job, son. You did more than I expected. Here, give me the paint and brushes. I'll take them to the garage. Just have a seat in the house."

When Dad came in the back door, the picket fence painter was pealing tomatoes for Mom and I was wearing a dress and had my hair done as well as I could in my hurry.

Mom said, "Jim, David has consented to be our guest for supper. As soon as we finish preparing the salad, we can eat, so go get washed up."

Dad left without a remark.

I watched David's hands and face. He was so intent. He paid no attention to me. I hadn't said a word at all to him yet.

After several minutes of silence in the kitchen, David stopped pealing tomatoes.

He said:

> "Thirteen and a baker's dozen
> were all you wished
> No more, no less
> than a dozen and one."

As Mom put her apron away, she said, "That will be fine, David. May I introduce you to my daughter, Jennifer?"

David looked at me, my hair, and

my dress.

He said:

> "It is my pleasure
> I knelt by you earlier
> with the flowers
> in their beds."

I said, "Hello, David.   How far did you walk?"

He said:

> "Miles I never count
> though it seemed not far at all
> when I saw you
> with the flowers
> and this job to do."

Dad came back into the kitchen and sat down at the table. I sat down.

Dad said, "Sit down, son."   Dad motioned to the chair opposite my own.

David sat down slowly looking at me, at my father, and at the setting of the table seemingly all at once.

Mom set the salad on the table near David.   She asked, "What do you think, David?"

He looked intently at the salad and then looked up at her.

He said:

"So it will mix is why
the insulating shell
is stolen away from the fruit.
The salad looks to me
like a flowered garden,
of gardenias and grass,
the world and
a blue-white fence
all come together."

Mom touched his shoulder gently and sat down.

Dad took my hand in one of his and held his other hand out to David. David took Dad's hand first and then Mom's. I saw in David's face that the moment pleased him beyond words he might not have expressed anyway.

Dad prayed, "Dear Lord, gracious is your gift of life and love to us. May we share as you have shared. Amen."

Dad placed a serving of potatoes on his plate and waited for me to serve myself a slice of meatloaf. Mom dipped out a serving of buttered corn onto her plate. Dad passed his plate to me; I passed my plate to Mom; and Mom held her plate out for David to take.

Mom said, "Have some salad, David and pass your plate."

I asked, "Dad, do you want a slice and a half of meatloaf?"

Dad answered, "Please."

After I served Dad some meatloaf from the serving dish in front of me, David understood. He served himself some salad and passed his plate to Dad. Then the merry-go-round of plates ran smoothly.

There was very little conversation at the supper table. David seemed reluctant to talk. Dad and Mom seemed unsure what questions were polite to ask him. I didn't say a word. Quietness was not my distinguishing characteristic, but David kept me shy.

Mom noticed when David had finished eating. She said, "You may be excused, David. We will have dessert later this evening."

Dad said, "That's fine with me, Amy. I already feel over indulged."

Mom and David left the table together.

I cleared the table and stacked the

dishes.   The dishes would be washed after it was too dark to see outside.   Dad was getting his pipe

Mom and David were on the porch talking when I came out.   Mom was sitting on the lawn chair near the railing. David was standing near the wall with his hands in his pockets.

I heard Mom say, "Be sure to walk down and see the pond before you go, David.   It is a delightful place for meditation."

She looked at me and stopped talking.   Mom smiled at me and said, "David is leaving soon."

I wished I'd heard more of their conversation.

David turned his head and looked at me.

Dad opened the door and stepped out of the house just then. He looked at David and then at me.

David said:

"I leave you with thankfulness
for the fence-painting
blue and white,
for the food and your kindness.

    I go before sunset
    blends me with my shadow."

Dad said, "David, you did a ten-dollar job in five. I will pay you that." Dad brought out his billfold and pulled out a bill.[7]

David looked at the ten dollars offered him for many moments. Then he took it and folded it into a square very, very small and placed it in the watch pocket of his jeans.

He said:
    "With permission
    I walk on my way
    I will see the pond you have
    beyond the clump of trees."

He left the porch and began to walk away and down the path.

I looked at my parents' faces. Dad just looked back at me without expression; Mom looked away.

Mom said, "You're twenty-one."

I looked at Dad. He was watching Mom and avoided my eyes.

I ran down the porch steps and

---

[7]The minimum wage back then was often one dollar an hour.

caught up with David as he followed the path that turned behind the garage. I took his arm.

When I could speak slowly without breathing too hard, I asked, "Where are you from, David?"

He said:

> "I suppose
> from where I choose
> if I chose."

I said, "That doesn't answer my question."

He said:

> "Your question was not
> the one you wanted truthfully
> an answer for."

I said, "Must you talk that way."

He said:

> "No
> though talking always seems
> to flow along like water
> moving over slimy covered
> rocks in a torpid stream."

I asked, "What was the question I wanted answered?"

He said:

> "Why or who I am

is unimportant.
Am I, is the question for
the mind full of apparent floors
looking strong yet drop beneath
the lightest treading quest
of answer."

He stopped speaking and I did not ask another question before we reached the pond.

I asked, "David, what did Mom say to you? Better yet, what did you say to Mom?"

He said:

"There was nothing spoken
by me. I'd just listen."

He looked at the water in the pond and his face seemed saddened. He was intent as he saw the pond. He seemed to want to look away.

I asked, "David, why did you come and see the pond?"

He said:

"To take leave.
Burning into me
there came an order.
Said: To water,
pool beyond the trees."

He looked at me intently. I felt my dress touching my skin; I felt my hair against the back of my neck; I felt my lips with my breath.

He touched my hair and freed it from my neck. He touched my lips and stole them from my breath. He placed an arm around my waist.

I had no dress but just the feel of his hand upon my back. I had a back, a warm back, a melting back that he molded in. I could not see; only feel and I felt my head bend back and his mouth on my throat. My arms were snakes coiling around him and vines of iron enfolding him.

And I heard him whisper while nibbling on my ear:

> "With my hands I marry you
> my Jennifer, to life.
> So long, long it was,
> had to be.
> Make me a memory
> and stay,
> be here untrue, unknowing
> with some other."

He pulled my arms down to my

sides and held them there another kiss.

I opened my eyes.

David was gone.

I was standing just where he left me with my arms down at my sides. As I turned to walk back alone, I looked down and saw the ten-dollar bill folded into a square very, very small, lying in the grass.[8]

---

[8] I wrote this in the spring of 1966 and asked a female friend to read it at the meeting of the Quiz and Quill. I wanted to find out if the group would think that she wrote it and not me. I wanted to know if I was I able to write from a woman's point of view. What do you think?

WHY IS THERE A RAINBOW?

"Why is there a rainbow?" you ask. I'm not sure your mind can actually comprehend the true reason for the phenomenon, but you will enjoy a fairytale story of how the first rainbow was made.

You see, many years ago – I believe a thousand or three – there lived in the sky beautiful people called gods. These gods had a city. I don't believe they ever referred to their city as "the New Jerusalem," but it was often called, the City of Gods or Mount Olympus.

Within this city, the gods lived very much like ordinary people. They had a government and a police force that were as corrupt as their Head God, the Big Stiff, President or Dictator off the City of Gods. This fellow, Jupiter by name, controlled every enterprise from star-making to marriages. And oh did that Jupiter love his women!

No goddess was safe out on the

streets night or day, except his wife. After a few scenes, goddesses were so scarce to the old boy that he would often leave his beloved city and find some leggy mortal woman.

Because of that, there were a lot of half-gods and half-goddesses running around half-naked through the forests of ancient Greece. But enough about him, we want to know about the very first rainbow.

Since the Big Stiff had a monopoly on the marriage bureau. He could marry any goddess to any god that he chose.

For some unknown reason, one day, a new goddess was created by the sea. The sea used its purest sea foam to create the goddess' body and its finest golden seaweed to make her hair. When the Head God saw this chick, he completely flipped. But that doll Venus would have nothing to do with him – he was a pretty old god.

Now Jupiter was angered that she would not sleep with him; he decided to avenge himself. He found the ugliest, most deformed god around and married

Venus to him

The ugly god, Vulcan, took Venus home with him. The poor girl couldn't bear to look at him; he was so ugly. For a woman as beautiful as Venus to be stuck with an ugly, lamed fellow like Vulcan was a crime – at least that is what Venus told herself. As a result, the newest goddess wouldn't let her husband get within ten feet of her; let alone, touch her.

Although Vulcan was the ugliest god living in those days, he was the kindest. He saw that his young and beautiful wife did not love him as Jupiter had told him. He was saddened; but he decided to let her have her way. He built her the most beautiful palace in the City of Gods; he made with his own hands: paintings, sculptures, furniture, and jewelry so beautiful that they could have been made for the use of only one goddess – Vulcan's lovely wife, Venus.

Vulcan stayed away from his wife and only saw her when he presented her with gifts of his design and construction. Venus was the best dressed (or undressed) goddess in the City of Gods. She was grateful to Vulcan, but she shuddered every time she thought of him touching her.

Since Venus was the sexiest, most alive goddess, she could hardly be expected to refrain from sleeping with a god every other night or so. She tried to remain faithful to that marriage, but Passion was the epitome of her being.

When the handsomest of all gods approached her with a proposition one evening, he took her bait. Yet Mars did not satisfy her longing for love. Passion in her was so bound up with love that she searched everywhere for a god or man who could assuage her need for love as well as her passion.

It was neither a satisfied nor a happy Venus who slept with a different god or man each night. Venus even slept with the Old Man, Jupiter himself. But the experience was so revolting that she rebounded by chasing Apollo for two years. Once he was trapped in bed, Apollo did not satisfy the inner craving of her soul either.

Poor Venus, she tried to find love with passion so often that she overplayed the percentages of her contraceptives being foolproof. She had several children she did not really want. Childbirth and raising children did not satisfy her inner desires; although she tried to lavish all the love she could upon these several children.

What did Vulcan do during all this time? – Nothing. He loved his wife so much that he gave her an unlimited charge account. And Venus spent the unlimited.

One day, Venus happened to be walking in the garden at a very unusual hour and found Vulcan pruning a rose bush. Venus said, "Hello," as softly and gently as she could for she felt miserable about breaking her marriage vow.

At the sound of her voice, Vulcan turned to look at her. The smile he gave her was the most beautiful smile Venus had ever seen. His ugly face lost all of its implied cruelty with that smile. That smile told her that he knew that she could not control herself.

Venus was so happy that tears seeped out of the corners of her eyes. Now, she felt free to look him straight in the eye; she had never felt so free before.

Venus saw in Vulcan's eyes his beautiful, magnificent soul laid bare. She saw the great love he had for her; she saw the scars of torture on his heart: scars of wounds she was unaware of inflicting each time she had slept with one of the other gods or with a man; she saw the infinite knowledge and understanding he had for her. Vulcan had no hate or jealousy in his soul, only love for his Venus.

She stepped toward him with her eyes on his soul. Vulcan made love to her there, on the bed of grass beside the rose bush.

Venus found with her husband that very special mixture of love and passion that she had been seeking everywhere.

Venus and Vulcan still had their middle age and old age to live together. They loved each other passionately. Their children were the loveliest and most intelligent in all the City of Gods.

Their first born entered politics and eventually instigated a revolution that overthrew Jupiter and established a true democracy. Venus and Vulcan were so proud.

Their marital happiness was written about by all the sages and used as an example for all god and goddess marriages. Everyone was kind enough to forget to the minutest detail all of the many years of scandal in their marriage.

And, oh yes, Venus discarded all her multicolored negligees that were relics of an unhappier time. She threw them out the window and all mortals below marveled at the beautiful band of color that curved across the sky as the negligees descended.[9]

---

[9] I wrote this in the fall of 1965 at Otterbein College when I wasn't on stage during rehearsals for a play. A couple members of the crew asked me what I was doing. I read it to them after it was finished. They said that they liked it and that I should write more of them. I found one more in my notes. It is entitled "A THING TO REMEMBER" and it can be found in my book, **ODDS AND ENDS: Stories and Essays from the Sixties.**

MOVIN' IN

When I got my letter of acceptance for college in March of 1963, I wrote back that I wanted a single room if at all possible. However, I was willing to have a roommate if a single room wasn't available. In August when I arrived at the dorm, I was given a key and told that my room was at the end of the third hallway to the left.

I hauled my stuff down to the room and opened the door. My roommate was already there.

He introduced himself. He said, "Hi, I'm Donald Hines. Everyone calls me Don."

I said, "Hi, I'm Robert Bowers and everyone calls me Rob."

We shook hands. There were two beds in the room and his stuff was already on the right side, so I moved into the closet and desk and bed on the left.

We had different schedules so I hardly ever saw him. I was taking an overload so I was often in classes until dark. We said, "Hi," to each other when we were in the room at the same time.

He never talked about himself and neither did I. I was too busy to make friends. I wanted to graduate in three years if at all possible. It had taken me three years to save up enough money to go to college. I had to make up the time somehow.

We lived this way for half a semester. Then the Junior Counselor stopped me in the hall to ask me how things were going. I said, "Fine. I don't see much of my roommate but we get along."

He laughed and said, "Roommate, you must be kidding. You have the only single room in this dorm."

I laughed and said, "I was kidding." Then I shut up and walked away. I was very confused.

When I opened the door to my room, Don was there. I said, "Don, I just met the Junior Counselor in the hall and he said this was a single room and I did not have a roommate. So who the hell are you?"

He nodded his head and said, "He's right. This is a single room. I moved in here in September 1958 and I have been here since then. You are the first roommate I have had in four years. None of the others ever stayed. Until you got here, I have been alone. Why didn't you leave when you found that the room was occupied?"

I answered, "I requested a single room but wrote that I would accept a roommate if a single room wasn't available. So I moved in."

He smiled and said, "I like you."

I said, "And I like you."

He said, "Sit down. Let me tell you a story."

I sat down at my desk chair and wheeled it around so I could face him. He sat cross-legged on his bed and told me his story.

He told me about working for four years and then coming to this college in

1958. He asked for a single room and got this room.

He really enjoyed the freedom of going to classes, being in cross-country in the fall and track in the spring. He met girls and dated some. In the fall of 1960, he met a freshman girl who was using a study carrel near his own. He began to have whispered conversations with her on occasion. She was shy and studious. Eventually he asked her on a date.

She told him that she was engaged to boy back home. He left her alone to study that day. Every day after that he always greeted her and they talked for a while before getting to their studies.

When he met her in the halls or on the sidewalks, he would walk along with her for a ways. Eventually he asked her to have a coke with him at the student center. She said yes and it was the first of many conversation dates over a coke, during a walk along the banks of the creek, and even sitting next to each other on a park bench.

In November, he told her that he

loved her.

She shook her head and said, "You can't love me. I'm nearly engaged to my guy back home."

He said, "Oh, but I do. I really love you."

She kept saying that he couldn't be in love with her and he mustn't talk about it or she would have to avoid him from then on. He was able to convince her that they could just be friends.

He didn't see her until after Thanksgiving break. The snow had fallen and he was on one of his solitary walks down by the lake. It was the first time he had ever seen her there.

She smiled as soon as she saw him. She said, "Kiss me! I've just been chosen as a candidate for Winter Homecoming Queen."

She held out her arms. He put his arms around her and kissed her; and he kissed her and he kissed her.

She responded with such wonder and surprise that she could respond to his kiss.

When they came up for air, she

said, "I've just been standing here, feeling good about myself and I saw you and I wanted to share my good feelings with you. I didn't know that I loved you so much until just now."

My roommate was ecstatic. He let go of her and literally danced with happiness there in the snow along the lake shore. Then they walked and talked along the parkway on the way back to her dorm.

While they were still out of sight of the campus buildings, she said, "Kiss me again. I don't believe it's true."

He kissed her and the same magic was there. He was so happy. When they broke from that kiss, he pranced and danced around and he didn't notice a car coming down that rarely used road. It hit him. It killed him.

I said, "How can you be here if you are dead?"

He said, "I don't know. I don't understand it. I am sure I am dead and yet I feel so alive. But when I leave this room, no one can see me. I have form and body only in this room.   I can communicate with you but to no one else – unless they come into this room."

I said, "I don't understand you. I am not sure that I believe you."

He said, "My God, I don't believe it either. But it must be true. I only seem to have a body during the day. You see me now, but tonight when it is dark, you will only be able to see me when you turn on the light."

I said again, "I don't believe you."

He said, "Wait! Wait until tonight and we will see."

We did. It was true. How, I don't know. He didn't know. He just knew that his girlfriend was still at school. Her name was Karyn. She was a senior and she was very sad and lonely as she completed her degree. She kept to herself and had no friends. She rarely spoke to anyone, unless spoken to.

He went to her all of the time, but he could not reach her or communicate with her. Her grief was so great that it shut out his attempts to touch her mind and thought. She wasn't open to his presence and she wasn't open to the presence of anybody else.

He asked me to help. I did.

Soon I found her, and tried to befriend her. She persistently tried to shut me out of her life.

My roommate had written poems and love letters for her, but none of them were corporate when he took them to her and left them in her room or at her study carrel in the library.

I rewrote them or typed them using his words and then I left them for her. Karyn began to respond to me as a friend.

He would talk to me in my mind and tell me what to say. At first, I thought he was speaking to me and I would answer him aloud. Eventually, I got accustomed to it and realized that he was simply trying to help me court her.

Finally Karyn went for a walk with me down by the lake. By then she trusted me as a friend and she told me about her lost love and she cried. I held her and comforted her. (He was with me when I held her. He could touch her through my body.)

When she was over her crying, she laid her head on my shoulder. As she quieted, he said, kiss her.

I hesitated.

He said, kiss her.

I kissed her forehead and then her eyes and her cheeks and her nose. When I kissed her mouth, he kissed her through me. She responded, clinging to me. It was wild, passionate.

We stroked and fondled each other. Soon we were lying down in the grass on my jacket. I entered her gently and she responded like a morning glory opening for the sunshine after a night of being closed up tight.

I couldn't believe it. It was so beautiful; so spontaneous; so tender.

It was May 9, 1964. A day I will always remember.

After I delivered her to her dormitory, I went to my room. My roommate wasn't there. I tried turning the lights on and off a number of times. He did not appear.

His bed was there. His clothes were in his closet. His books were there. His papers, pens, chair and desk were there, but he wasn't.

My bed was there. My books were there. My desk and chair were there. And my clothes were in the closet. But he wasn't there.

I kept seeing his girl (my girl now?) every moment I could and she was so happy.

Since I was still in school, Karyn got a teaching job in the area for the fall. She rented an apartment in town as of June 3, 1964. It was unfurnished except for stove and refrigerator. She would occupy it in July, after spending a couple of weeks with her parents, telling them about our planned marriage.

I had never mentioned the subject. But touching her was a beautiful experience and I wasn't going to say no.

In the meantime, I was studying for finals and trying to figure out where in the hell was my roommate.

When the time came for me to move out of the dorm for the summer, I decided to move into our apartment instead of moving back home. Once my stuff was moved into the apartment, I turned in my dorm key to the Junior Counselor. Then he went with me to inspect my dorm room. I was hoping to get a refund of my deposit.

We walked into my dorm room and he saw the clothes and books and bed clothes and towels. He said, "How come you haven't moved your stuff out of this room?"

I said, "I did. You saw me move out. This stuff belongs to my roommate."

He said, "Come on, don't give me that."

I said, "Look, you saw me moving out with my books, clothes, and suitcases. This stuff isn't mine."

He said, "This room was empty of all this stuff last August. You are the only person who has been in this room all year. If you don't claim this stuff, who does it belong to?"

He reached over for a book and looked inside. He said, "Right here it says that this book belongs to Donald

Hines. Who is that? I've never heard of him."

I said, "Donald Hines is my roommate."

He asked, "Then all these clothes in the closet are his too?"

I said, "Yes."

He asked, "Where is your roommate?"

I said, "I haven't seen him for a month."

He looked at the size of the shirts in the closet. He said, "15 ½ - 33. What size do you wear?"

I said, "The same."

He read, "Pants size 30 – 30."

I said, "The same. But how can that be? Donald Hines was four inches taller than I am and he weighed twenty more pounds."

The Junior Counselor said, "I don't want to hear anymore about it. Even if your name isn't in the books, these must be your clothes."

I said, "I don't understand it. My roommate had such a different taste in clothes, even if they are my size."

He said, "Maybe you should see the counselor at the student medical center."

I said, "Forget it. I'll move the stuff out." And I did.

But where in the hell was my roommate?

I was moved out of the dorm and into the apartment. Karyn moved in with me, but she didn't turn in her dorm room key in order to keep up appearances.

We were sleeping on the floor of the living room on the thick carpet. We didn't have the money to buy a bed or a mattress.

I began to wear my roommate's clothes to try them out. Her parents were coming for her graduation. Today was Thursday. They would be coming Friday evening. That was tomorrow night.

We were making love. That seemed to be all we had done since we moved in together. I was feeling like a split personality: Involved and watching it at the same time.

Finally I couldn't keep silent anymore. I was overcome with a feeling of tremendous sadness and I began to cry.

Karyn was on top, straddling me. She stopped moving and lay down pressing her warm naked body against me.

She held me and asked, "What's wrong?"

I told her everything.

She was shocked. She grew rigid. It was my turn to hold her, but she pulled away and sat up. She just stared at me for a while. Then she began to tremble and shake.

I grabbed her and pulled her down beside me and I held her.

After a few minutes, she raised her head from my shoulder and put her hands around my neck. She looked me in the eye. She had such beautiful brown and green eyes.

She asked, "Do you love me?"

A part of me wanted to shout, "Yes! Yes! I love you." But another part of me said, "I don't know. I don't understand what's happening."

She said, "Show me the books."

We opened all of the boxes holding his stuff. We looked in every book at the marginal notes and the underlining. We looked through the papers and poems and short stories.

I began to feel dizzy. We fixed some coffee. Then we looked through my books and papers.

His textbooks and paperbacks were all copyrighted in 1958 or earlier. Some of my books were copyrighted later.

Karyn said, "Here, write me a note."

I took the paper and pen and sat down on the floor and wrote using a box of books for a desk. I wrote:

I love you, my darling.
I love you, my sweet.

And it went on from there. It was a long letter; it was a poem. I didn't think about it; I just wrote it. Then I handed it to her without reading it.

She read it through and looked at me thoughtfully. She took note papers from my stuff and note papers from my roommate's stuff.

She said, "Come here."

She lay down on her stomach on our bed of blankets and sheets. She put all of the papers in two piles in front of her.

I lay down beside her.

She held up the note I had just written and said, "Look! Whose handwriting is this?"

I looked. It was my roommate's handwriting.

I said, "Oh, God, Karyn, I am feeling very confused."

She began to rub my back and I tried to relax with my head down and my eyes closed.

After a while, she rolled me over onto my back and took me into her mouth. When I had an erection, she made love to me.

Karyn looked beautiful in her cap and gown.

Her parents stayed at a motel. They were nice people.

Sunday after graduation, we went

home with them.

Officially Karyn slept in her room with her sister, Josephine. I slept in the guest room. At night after her parents were asleep, Karyn slept with me.

We couldn't be separated for very long. We seemed to need physical contact. It was a tremendous hunger in both of us.

After the fourth of July, we returned to our apartment and got used furniture from Goodwill. We got a card table and chairs, a lamp, an end table for the lamp, and a desk that we would share. We still couldn't afford a bed.

I wrote to my parents, but I was afraid to go home. I needed to resolve who I was and what was happening in my mind. And I didn't want to leave Karyn.

Eventually Karyn convinced me that I should go home and see what happened. She went with me so I wouldn't be alone with whatever may occur. We took the bus.

Nothing happened. My love for Karyn was ever present.

My parents' only comment was to Karyn when I was out visiting some high school friends and they were alone together: "He seems so happy and content. He laughs more and doesn't seem so tense and irritable."

When we left my home for the return trip to our apartment, we took the bus again. I was feeling less ambivalent and more together. And yet, something was still missing.

It was July 27, 1964. Karyn was gone from the apartment. She was shopping for groceries.

I was doing some writing. I was doing a paper for summer school. Suddenly the continuity of what I was writing was broken by these words:

Karyn is mine!

You can't have her!

My hand wrote those words. After I read them, I blacked out.

When I regained consciousness, I was lying on the floor next to the desk and someone was sitting in the chair and watching me. It was Donald Hines, my roommate.   There were tears in his eyes.

I sat up and leaned back against the desk. We began to talk.

He said, "You are shutting me out of Karyn's life!"

I said, "Don, I wouldn't even know Karyn if it weren't for you. You got me to meet her, to court her, and to love her. She wouldn't even have responded to me if you hadn't been part of my experience of her."

He said, "And now you are shutting me out! Now you are making love to her all the time and all I can do is watch!"

I said, "It doesn't have to be like that, Don. You can be a part of us too."

He said, "No, I can't. I'm dead. There's no way for me to live in you. You've taken Karyn from me."

I said, "Before I knew your true nature, Don, I liked you. You felt that didn't you? I've learned to love who you are and all your interests and feelings. I appreciate you.   I would incorporate you, if you will let me."

He said, "I don't want to be a part of you. I want to be you. And I want to do it as myself. I want Karyn!"

I said, "Aw! Damn it, Don! There is no way you can be me. But I'm willing to share my life with you. I want you to be a part of me. I want to be part of you. I am a part of you. Karyn is more you than me, but I love her. I share her with you. I kiss her, taste her, and smell her as both of us, not just myself."

He stood up and said, "I can't do it. I can't give her up! And if I can't have her, you can't either."

I asked, "What are you going to do?"

He answered, "If I can't share her life, I'll share her death!" He walked toward the door.

I said, "No you don't! Karyn is alive and open with me now. And I will keep her free."

He started to run, but I dove for him and caught him by the door. He kicked me in the face and just about knocked me silly.

He shouted, "I'll take care of that

unfaithful bitch! She'll be cold to you, dead and cold."

I shouted back, "By God you won't! You had her shut tight and frozen for three years! That's enough. She is warm now. Alive! Willing to risk getting hurt again! You'll leave her alone, or you will share her with me."

We rolled around on the floor, grunting and cursing. We knocked over the lamp and a couple of chairs and the card table with the noon dishes on it. They fell and shattered on the tile of the kitchen floor.

He got his hands around my neck and started to choke me. I got to my knees and rammed him against the wall with my shoulder. He kept the choke hold on me. I got to my feet and kneed him in the crotch. He kept on cutting off my breath. Keeping him tight against the wall with the pressure of my weight, I brought up my hands and pried his fingers from my throat. Slowly I was able to pin his arms down and hold him there.

I don't know how long I held him

there. I knew I couldn't let go. Karyn's life was at stake. It seemed like hours. I was tiring, but so was he.

The key sounded in the door. I tried to call out: Karyn, don't come in! But the words wouldn't come out.

Don struggled harder and kicked out with his knees. But I held on.

The door opened and Karyn came into the room.

Don seemed to melt between my arms; melt into my own body until I was standing and pressing my face and body against the wall.

Karyn looked at me and asked, "What are you doing?" She looked around the room and asked, "What happened?"

I smiled at her and came at her with a gleam in my eye. She backed away from me but not fast enough. I caught her and picked her up in my arms and spun around, dancing with her.

I said, "I just won an argument with myself. I'll tell you about it later."

I kissed her and she responded wildly. I don't remember how we got our clothes off and managed to get to the bed made up on the floor. We made love; true love, more beautiful and passionate and mindless than anytime I could remember.

We didn't even realize that we had left the apartment door open until we heard our landlady yell in the doorway: "Who let this ice cream melt all over the carpet out here in the hall?"

Karyn yelped, "Oh! I left the groceries in the hall."

And she left right in the middle of the action and ran out of the door as naked and beautiful as . . .

(I just can't describe her.)

And the landlady fainted.[10]

---

[10] I wrote this in 1963 shortly after arriving at Otterbein College and meeting my roommate in the freshman dormitory.

COME PLAY WITH ME

"Rob, go out and play." His mother suggested.

"Yes, Mother."

Rob sighed. He sat cross-legged by the large bookcase. He was half-hidden by a plush armchair. He had the "A" encyclopedia open on his lap. He reluctantly closed the book on "aardvark".

"Rob, did you hear me!" his mother wondered.

Rob poked his head out from behind the plush chair.

He said, "Yes, Mother."

His mother was busy directing the maids. She was having a mid-morning tea, today. She didn't want an eight-year-old boy around while the house was prepared.

Rob got to his knees and replaced the book on the shelf where he had found it. Someone was always disarranging the encyclopedia. Rob didn't have time to rearrange the books in alphabetical order now; he would do that later.

He clambered to his feet and walked out of the room, carefully bypassing his mother and the working maids. He headed toward the kitchen.

He faintly heard the comment his mother made about him to the maids, "That boy is always underfoot!"

"Yes, Ma'am," came the chorused response from the three maids. They always agreed with Madame anyway.

Rob pushed open the swinging door and entered the kitchen. The cook looked around from behind the counter. She saw him and smiled.

She said, "Hello, Robbie."

The cook was the only one of the servants who really ever acknowledged his existence. Madame hardly ever entered the kitchen. The cook was as free as anyone could be in this house. She chose to notice Rob and speak to him. She called him Robbie; his mother called him Rob; the other servants answered his questions with "Yes, or no,

Master Robert."

The cook asked, "Going out to look at the garden?"

Rob nodded his head. He rarely said anything.

The cook gave him a large slice of raw pastry. Rob smiled his thanks and took a small bite as he started out the servants' entrance.

She said, "Come back and tell me how the roses smell and count the number of blossoms. There will be more today. Pick one for me, Robbie."

Rob said, "I will, Carrie."

He looked behind him. The cook was busy behind the counter. She was always working. He never understood why she bothered to speak to him.

Rob was outside looking at the row of cars the servants brought each morning. There was a nine-passenger station wagon, (Carrie drove that.) several sedans and the sports car that the head butler owned.

Rob walked past the first five cars and stopped at the light blue station wagon. He stuck his head in the open window. There was a doll lying on the first backseat.

Rob hadn't known that Carrie was married and had children. She must take her wedding ring off when she works, Rob decided, and Carrie has a little girl who plays with dolls.

The first doll Rob had seen was one that his cousin brought with her when his father's brother and sister-in-law came for a short visit. They stayed four days. His cousin had talked him into doing a lot of things he shouldn't have done. It had been fun, though.

Rob left the cars behind and walked into the garden. He smelled the roses. He would tell Carrie that they smelled like her hair. Then Carrie would stop working and bend down and kiss him. Rob liked her to do that. Her kiss was gentle and very soothing on his cheek.

Rob counted the blossoms: there were twenty blooming roses on that bush. He counted the rose buds and was pricked by the thorns as he made sure that he missed none. There were thirteen rosebuds; a few were about to bloom. Tomorrow they might be open.

Rob looked for the youngest and prettiest rose blossom. He wouldn't pick it now. He would wait until he was ready to go in.

The longer he stayed out this morning; the better his mother would like it. Her tea would not be over until after his lunchtime. He would not be allowed to eat until the tea was over. Carrie would have a sandwich ready for him if he got hungry before then. He would bring it outside to eat it. The sandwich would hold him until his delayed lunchtime.

Rob smelled the rose he had chosen one more time, thinking of what he would tell Carrie. He left the trellis and walked toward his swing.

He had wanted a swing like the picture of one that he saw in one of his books. He had looked for a tree for his swing and found one in a corner formed by the high stone wall around the estate. The grass was very soft and green in that corner and the tree was the biggest in the yard.

He had asked Carrie what to use to make a swing. The cook brought him a length of heavy rope the next day.

He made his own swing using a board he found in the gardener's tool shed for the seat.

Rob came out of the garden and walked around the shrubbery. He made ready to run to his swing.

It wasn't there. There were two ends of rope hanging down from the high limb; they weren't very long.

Rob felt about to cry, but he didn't. His father told him boys shouldn't cry. He never cried now even when his father took the strap to him. If he didn't cry when his father hurt him, he certainly wasn't going to cry because his swing was gone.

Rob walked toward the tree. He stood below the limb looking up. He would climb up and tie the ropes together.

He looked around for the torn rope. He saw it in a pile of debris by the wall. The rope was cut into six inch pieces; the board was only broken splinters.

No, Rob told himself, I won't cry!

It was no secret now how the swing was destroyed. The gardener had done it.

Rob wasn't allowed to have dangerous toys and, of course, a swing that would carry a boy as high as or higher than the wall was dangerous. His father had probably told the gardener what to do.

Rob wasn't bitter; he was just disappointed that he could not keep the swing longer. He would have preferred feeling his father's strap to having his swing destroyed like that.

Rob sat down on the grass under the tree and closed his eyes. He couldn't tie the rope back together. If he told Carrie what happened, the cook would only bring him another rope. Rob wouldn't tell Carrie; she might lose her job if he did. He wanted Carrie more than he wanted the swing.

Rob told himself, "I could always go to the play gym and swing. But it's an awfully small swing and it doesn't go very high."

Rob leaned back on the grass and spread his arms and legs wide. He lay there under the tree a long time thinking of something to do.

He could go swimming naked in the garden pool like he had done with his cousin. No, that wasn't any fun to do alone. One needed to swim with a friend. Rob had tried swimming alone once before; he hadn't enjoyed it.

Rob rolled over onto his stomach and chewed on an available blade of grass. After a while, the blade of grass was bitten in two and he spat it out of his mouth.

He had a brainstorm. He could play with the echo! He stood up and faced the corner of the wall.

He called out, "Hello!"

"Hello!" answered the echo.

"What's your name?" Rob called.

"What's your name?" said Echo.

"Well," began Rob.

"Well," began Echo.

"My name is Rob." Rob said.

"My name is Rob," replied Echo.

"What a coincidence!" Rob called.

"What a coincidence!" said Echo.

"I'm lonely." Rob said.

"I'm lonely," Echo called back.

"Come play with me." Rob asked.

"Come play with me," copied Echo.

"I will." Rob answered.

"I will," the echo repeated.

"One of these days," Rob said so low that the echo didn't hear and mock him.

Rob did not speak for a few minutes. Then he started again, "Hello!"

"Hello!" answered two echoes.

"Who's on the other side of that wall?" the echo asked.

"I am!" Rob answered.

"I am!" the echo repeated.

"What's your name?" the echo asked.

"Rob!" Rob answered.

"Rob" the echo repeated.

"My name is Chris!" the echo said.

"Chris?" Rob echoed.

"Chris?" the echo echoed.

"Yes!" the echo said.

Rob didn't say anything. He began to climb the tree. It took him awhile although he hurried as fast as he could. He climbed as high as he could go and he looked down over the wall. A boy the same age as Rob stood on the other side staring at the wall.

"Hello!" Rob called down.

The other boy looked up and said, "Hello!"

Rob said, "Gee! I thought I was imagining things.

Rob climbed down to the branch that overhung the wall. He walked out on the limb until he was right above the top of the wall. He sat down on the branch with his legs on either side. He leaned forward and wrapped his arms around the branch, slid his legs off of it until he turned over and hung upside-down. Then he held onto the branch, brought his legs down, and let them dangle above the wall. Still holding onto the branch, he lowered himself carefully to the top of the wall. Then he sat down and hung his legs over the other side.

Chris had watched all of this silently.

Rob asked, "What are you doing

here?" He said that while looking at the woods and the meadow that seemed to stretch endlessly on the side of the wall where the other boy stood looking up.

Chris answered, "My parents are stopped at a roadside park over there." He turned and pointed toward a hill full of trees in the distance. He added, "You can't see it from here. There's a freeway over there. It's got three lanes on each side of the road. It is the biggest expressway I have ever seen."

Rob said, "I know what an expressway is. I've been on one before. But what is a roadside park?"

Chris looked up at the boy sitting on the wall. Everybody knew what a roadside park was! Chris almost said so, but he remembered the wall. Maybe someone who lived behind a wall like that wouldn't know about roadside parks. He wondered if people living in East Berlin knew about roadside parks.

Chris said, "A roadside park is a park that is along the side a road. It has toilets and tables. It's a place where people can stop to eat lunch and go to the bathroom."

Rob said, "When I rode on the expressway, we stopped at a restaurant. I've never seen a roadside park. I know what a park is. A roadside park would be a park by the side of a road, wouldn't it?"

Chris agreed, "Yes, of course."

Rob said, "Do you think you could climb this wall?"

Chris looked up at the height of the wall and said, "It's very high."

Rob said, "I've never been where you are."

Chris was very interested in what might be on the other side of the wall.

Chris looked around. There were no trees he could climb to look over the wall. There were crevices in the wall. He might just be able to climb up to the top. His parents were napping after staying awake while his father drove all night. He wouldn't be expected until time for lunch or later.

Chris thought about the wall. He took off his shoes and socks, rolled up his jeans and approached the wall. It was very high. He had to strain his neck to see the boy sitting above him.

Chris put his toe on a projecting rock at the base of the wall. He found hand-holds above his head. He began to climb. His ascent was both vertical and diagonal.

When both boys sat upon the wall looking down, the view was more than Chris expected.

Chris said, "Golly, I didn't know that bunch of trees I passed through was so pretty!"

Rob said, "Someday I'll walk up that hill down there and through the trees and visit that roadside park."

Chris said, "I had to climb over a barbed wire fence to get here. There were many 'Do Not Trespass' signs hanging on it. Do you own all of that land?"

Rob answered, "I don't own anything, but my father might own all of that land."

Chris said, "Wow!"

Rob pointed to his parents' home and said, "That's the house I live in."

Chris said, "Wow!"

Rob said, "I'll show you around, Chris, but we will have to be very quiet. Mother is having a tea and she doesn't like disturbances."

Chris said, "Rob, you must be very rich."

Rob said, "I guess my parents are rich." He stood up on top of the wall and said, "Come on."

Rob grabbed a hold of the branch and pulled himself carefully onto it. He went down its length toward the trunk. Chris followed just behind him.

When they got to the ropes hanging from a limb, Rob said, "I had a swing until the gardener cut it down."

Chris said, "That must have been a good swing. I'll bet you could swing over the wall."

Rob said, "I could touch the top of it with my feet. If I made another one, they would cut it down too. At least I still have this tree to climb."

The boys went all over the private grounds. Rob told Chris about the roses and his encyclopedia. Chris told Rob about his trip to the New York World's Fair and all the things he saw.

The two boys hid like outlaws behind and beneath shrubs whenever the gardener passed near them. They crept as silently as Indians across the front lawn so they couldn't be seen from the house or by the watchmen at the front gate.

Keeping a lookout for the gardener or anyone else, the two boys stripped and played in the garden pool. They had to be careful about the water lilies, but otherwise they were as rowdy as they could get without making much noise.

It was as they lay side by side in the grass drying themselves in the heat of the sun that Rob commented on a phenomenon that had made him curious.

Rob asked, "Why do you have such dark skin all over your body?"

Chris looked at his new friend and asked, "Why do you have such white skin all over your body?"

Rob answered, "I guess I was born with it, except where I am tanned."

Chris said, "That answers your own question."

Rob sat up and looked over at his curly-haired friend and said, "You mean you were born with dark skin?"

Chris answered, "Yes. I'm a Negro."

Rob said, "Oh."

They didn't speak of the difference in their skin pigmentation again. The knowledge that one was born white and the other dark did not deter the boys from continuing the same warmth of friendship they had developed since they met.

When it was lunchtime, Rob told his friend to wait for him. Then Rob ran to the servants' entrance and entered the kitchen. He forgot all about the rose he planned to bring to the cook. Carrie had a sandwich waiting for him.

Rob accepted the sandwich and asked for one more. He said, "I have a friend."

Carrie said, "Certainly, you may have another, Robbie."

Carrie had two slices of bread out when footsteps from the main part of the house came toward the kitchen.

Rob said, "Someone's coming."

Carrie took the sandwich from Rob's hand and deftly cut it in two, diagonally. She handed the two halves to Rob. He took them and ran out the door.

The two boys sat in the tree in the corner by the wall and ate. They ate slowly, savoring each bite of the peanut butter and jelly sandwich. Chris ate one half; Rob ate one half.

After the sandwich was gone, the two boys sat on the wall and talked for thirty minutes. Then Rob pointed out the hand-holds and foot-holds as Chris climbed back down the outside of the wall.

Chris got back into his socks and shoes. Then he waved goodbye and headed across the meadow toward the roadside park hidden by the trees.

Rob watched his friend cross the meadow and climb the hill with all the trees on it. Just before Chris stepped into the woods, he paused and waved goodbye to Rob. Rob stood up on the wall and waved back. Chris turned his back and was soon lost to view.

Rob stayed on the wall for some time, staring after his friend. After a while, Rob climbed up as high as he could in the tree and looked carefully for a sight of the expressway, a view of the roadside park, or just the top of a car or truck traveling somewhere. Then he climbed down the tree and went into the house.

When Rob entered the kitchen, Carrie was busy with preparations for a dinner that evening. Before she left at five o'clock every day, dinner would be ready for the maids to serve whenever the mistress of the house determined.

Carrie noticed Rob immediately. He held out the rose for her with both hands. Carrie stopped what she was doing and took his hands in hers. She bent down and smelled the delicate fragrance of the rose. She said, "I know. It smells like my hair."

Rob nodded, but he could not smile.

Carrie kissed his forehead and each of his cheeks. Then she took the rose and hugged him tight. She whispered into his ear, "Thank you, Robbie, for the beautiful rose."

Rob whispered back, "Thank you for the two sandwiches, Carrie."

As Carrie smoothed his uncombed hair into place, she said, "Your mother has been waiting for you in the dining room, Robbie. Go to her at once."

When Rob entered the dining room, he saw his mother pacing about the room. She heard him enter and turned to look at him. She saw his grass-stained pants and shirt. His face was clean and so were his hands.

She said, "Where have you been?"

Rob answered, "Outside, Mother."

She said, "You have kept your lunch waiting, but that is pardonable. At least you did not disturb my tea."

Rob and his mother sat down at the table. His mother was eating nothing; she had eaten enough at the tea. She sat across from him and told him all about her tea as he ate.

When she was finally finished talking, Rob was eating dessert. She began to ask what he had been doing all morning.

Rob interrupted her. Rob asked, "What is a Negro, Mother?"

His mother looked at him with a shocked expression. She said, "Negroes are very nasty evil people with black skins."

Rob didn't say a word. He thought to himself, "How wrong you are, Mother. How wrong you are." And nothing ever changed his mind.[11]

---

[11] I wrote this in 1960 before the Black Power movement.

FINAL DECISION

Kathy sat in the fourth seat of the second row. She watched the instructor diagramming on the blackboard. She copied the diagram exactly on her note paper and placed notations beside it as she drew. The instructor finished the diagram and turned to face the class. The bell ending class rang.

The professor said, "We will resume the lecture at this point when class reconvenes on Monday. During the weekend, study the diagram. I may quiz you on its significance before resuming the lecture. Dismissed."

The Prof was out of the classroom before any of her students were out of their seats. She poked her head back into the room just as the deluge was about to pour into the hall.

Before she disappeared from view, Prof said, "Have a nice weekend."

"We will, Prof!" the first few students called down the hall after her.

Kathy was the last student out of the room. She turned off the lights and closed the door. Holding her books in front of her with both arms, she made her leisurely way down the hall. She opened the outside door and descended the six steps. She was heading toward the dormitory.

"Kathy!" called a familiar soft voice.

She turned around to face the group of trees in the center of the lawn. A man waved to her. He was sitting down, leaning against a tree.

She thought: He's probably been waiting for me.

Kathy walked across the grass. He stood up to greet her.

She said, "David, are you cutting your class again?"

David laughed. He looked around to see if anyone was looking in their direction. No one! He kissed her mouth gently, possessively. He bent down and picked up his books. He stood up beside her again.

He said, "Give me your books. I'll carry them"

She said, "No. You have enough of your own to carry."

The two of them walked toward the senior women's dormitory. Kathy waited for him to answer her question. They commented to each other about the weather. Finally David answered her question.

He said, "We had no class. The Reverend Mr. Frank Blair was called out of town to say goodbye to a corpse."

Kathy looked up into his twinkling blue eyes. She laughed and said, "David, you'll never change."

David said sadly, "I try, Kathy."

She pleaded, "Don't try too hard. I like your sense of humor."

David said, "You and only a few others." He changed the subject, "I've got tickets for this evening's performance of King Lear.

She said, "I'm sorry, D. My sorority has a special meeting tonight. I need to be there. The president just doesn't postpone the meetings she calls."

David said, "That's alright, K. I really didn't feel disposed to sit through that gruesome play anyway."

(They often used 'D' and 'K', the first letters in their names, as their pet names for one another.)

She asked, "You didn't buy those tickets, did you?"

He said, "You always are one to think of finances. No, I didn't. Professor King gave them to me."

She said, "How did you happen to see him?"

He answered, "He was the special lecturer at the seminary this afternoon for my class on pastoral care."

She said, "He's leaving for Washington, D. C. tonight, isn't he?"

He said, "Yes. That's why he gave me the tickets. He wasn't going to use them."

She said, "You could cash them in."

He said, "I could but I won't. Here, you give them to someone who wants them at supper tonight."

She asked, "You won't eat with me?"

He said, "Not this evening. I want to think for a few hours."

They stood at the door leading into the sitting room of the dorm.

She said, "You won't come in for a while?"

He said, "No, I'd rather not."

David opened the door for Kathy. She stepped into the building. David grabbed a hold of her arm and pulled her out again.

Kathy looked up at him. His soft, brown hair was windblown out of place.

Kathy laughed and said, "You appear entirely ferocious, David."

He said, "Well, this time you are correct. I do want you tonight."

Kathy stuck her nose up and looked at him with a condescending air and said with a My-Fair-Lady accent, "Well you can't have me."

He looked at her for a moment; then he said, "I'll see you tomorrow for lunch." He pushed her into the building and turned and walked down the stairs.

Kathy turned and called, "D?"

David didn't turn around.

Kathy set her books down and ran down the stairs after him. He didn't hear her call him and didn't hear her come up behind him. He was standing at the edge of the street.

She peeked around him and looked up into his face.

He was frowning, lost in thought. He saw her immediately and his face lost its furrows and he smiled at her.

She said, "I called you, D."

He said, "I'm sorry, K. I must not have heard you."

She asked, "What's troubling you?"

He answered, "A little problem that kept me awake for a long time last night." He was near tears.

She put her hands on his shoulders. She saw the tenseness of his mind in his blue eyes. She pulled his head down and kissed him.

He wasn't responsive for a second and then he dropped his books and was kissing her all over her face with the passion that he felt for her.

After a while, she stopped kissing him and whispered, "I'll see you tonight at eleven o'clock. I'll sign out for the weekend."

By midnight that evening, Kathy and David were together in a suite at a certain hotel of the university town. They sat together on the couch and watched what was left of the eleven o'clock news. Then they watched half of the first late night move. They were both a little nervous about being there.

At the next commercial, Kathy got up and turned off the television. David got up and walked toward the television set. Kathy stood in front of the screen and wouldn't move.

David said, "Let's . . ." He didn't get to finish his sentence. Kathy interrupted him.

She said, "No more diversions, D. You wanted me tonight for one purpose. That's why I talked you into bringing me here. Now let's begin."

He peered into her calm brown eyes. He slipped his hands behind her back and pulled her against him.

He said, "You are the funniest." He kissed her firmly. Then he said, "But why did we need to come here to discuss the problem?"

She wrinkled her nose at him and said, "Because a setting of this sort has much to do with our problem."

David noticed that she stressed the "our" that preceded "problem." He held her tightly against him because he knew that she had guessed his reason for wanting her with him. He was sure that she was trying to face a similar solution to their problem.

He placed an arm beneath her legs and picked her up. He carried her to the couch and lay her down with her head on two pillows. He took her hand and caressed it. Then he bent down and kissed her soft cheek. He sat on the very edge of the couch.

Kathy looked up into his sun-browned face. She whispered, "I love you, David."

He said, "Please don't say that, Kathy. I'd rather not think about it."

She said, "Why shouldn't I say it? I'll say it as often as I want!"

David caressed her cheek with the back of his hand. His other hand was held tightly between her two hands and pressed against her breasts.

David ran his free hand through her hair to the back of her head in a caress. He massaged the back of her neck. He said, "Now you are the one who is acting irrationally, K."

She released his hand. He left it there and gently rubbed a nipple through her blouse and bra. She moved her hands down to her sides. She stared up at the ceiling.

David pushed her hair away from her ear and kissed its lobe. His head moved slowly as he kissed his way down her neck. He planted the last kiss on her collar bone.

Kathy looked at him and said, "Oh, D. It would be so easy to undress and do what I want, but I won't."

David unbuttoned the top button of her blouse; and then another. One more button came out of its buttonhole before she took both of his wrists in her hands. She kissed each of his hands.

She said, "You'd do it too." Her tone was that of a mother speaking to her child.

David sighed and unclamped her hands from his wrists. He slid off the edge of the couch. He leaned his back against the couch and his head against her side.

Her hand gently tousled his soft hair. A shiver ran down his spine and he captured her hand with one of his before she caressed him too much.

David said, "It's been four years since I met you. We haven't dated anyone else for the last three years."

She said, "It's been nice knowing you."

David looked over his shoulder at her face. They laughed together.

David asked, "What was your sorority meeting about tonight?"

She said, "Mostly it was about the plans for the tea on Alumni Day, a week before graduation."

He asked, "Did you need to assess the sisters for more working capital?"

She said, "Yes; and I remember you told me so."

She sat up and put both arms

around his neck. She held her cheek against the top of his head.

She said, "Oh, David, what are we going to do?"

He said, "I had pretty much decided what I should do, but the final decision is ours. We both need to agree upon a solution."

She said, "I knew that's why you wanted me tonight."

He turned his head and nuzzled her arm. Then he whispered, "Well, what shall we do, K?"

She said, "I've thought about it and thought about it until I get a headache. When did you first think of our problem?"

"Before I met you; maybe five years ago. Then it was just a theoretical problem."

She said, "And you never mentioned it to me?"

He asked, "Did you ever speak of it to me?"

She answered, "No. I . . . I didn't want to believe in its reality." She leaned back against the pillows and covered her face with her hands.

David stood up and bowed his head over her. Her white brassier was visible because she had not re-buttoned her blouse. David pulled her blouse back together and re-buttoned it.

Kathy did not move as he touched her. Her hands still covered her face and moisture was seeping beneath her hands and running down her cheeks to her neck.

David knew that she was crying and was certain that she did not want him to know. He left her side and went into the bedroom. He removed his shoes and lay down on the double bed. He closed his eyes, trying not to think; yet desiring to think.

David awoke with a start. How long had he been sleeping? He didn't know. He quickly climbed off of the bed and tiptoed into the other room.

Everything was as he had left it. The lights were on and Kathy was still lying on the couch. Her hands were clasped together and held against her cheek. She was asleep.

David turned out the light and then he tiptoed back into the bedroom and pulled the bedspread off of the bed. He returned to Kathy and covered her. As he tucked the bedspread around her, she aroused.

She whispered, "David?" And she reached out searching for him with her hands.

He knelt beside her and said, "Yes, Kathy?"

Her voice choking with her emotion, she said, "Oh, David."

He allowed her to bring his head down. She kissed his lips firmly, but with only a hint of passion.

David said, "I love you, K."

David kissed her damp forehead and went into the bedroom. He choked back his sobbing, but could not hold back his crying. He cried silently, inwardly, his eyes shedding many tears.

The next morning, he stepped into the bathroom without looking in on Kathy. He was shaving when Kathy came to the door and opened it.

She said, "May I watch you shave?"

He didn't answer.

She leaned back against the doorjamb and watched him using the safety razor.

David looked at her. Her face was streaked with last night's tears. Her voice was cheerful, but her soiled face was a noticeable contradiction to that cheerfulness. Although he attempted to ignore her presence, his eyes would find her face in the mirror after every stroke.

He finished shaving and rinsed a washcloth with warm water. He wrung it out and stepped over to Kathy.

She looked into his eyes. His eyes and face were grave.

She took the washcloth out of his hands and used it to wipe her face and neck. When she was finished, David pulled her against him and he kissed her mouth and cheeks and her closed eyelids and then her mouth again.

She did not respond to his kisses.

David smiled at her and said, "Cool as a cucumber, huh?"

She said, "No," and kissed a small bleeding cut on his jaw. Then she pushed him out of the bathroom and said, "Now it's my turn to take a shower."

He said, "Wait a minute, K, let me wash off this lather first."

She put a finger up and wiped off some shaving cream from his ear. She laughed and said, "You do have more on you! Finish washing while I get my clothes ready for today."

David was tying his tie in front of the mirror above the dresser in the bedroom when Kathy walked back through the bedroom toward the bathroom.

She stopped before the door and said, "We never finished our talk last night, did we?"

David looked up at her reflection in the mirror and said, "No, we didn't."

She said, "We will finish it today." Then she stepped into the bathroom and closed the door.

David did not hear her turn the lock. He knew that she had left the door unlocked on purpose. He was afraid to accept her invitation.

The shower began to run and he heard her gentle, alto voice singing "Autumn Leaves."

He retied his tie. The shower stopped.

She called, "David."

He heard her voice behind him. He said, "Yes?"

She said, "Will you get my slip out of my suitcase please? I forgot it."

He turned to look at her. He could see her naked body dripping wet behind the door. She held a towel in front of her. It partially hid her body from view.

David bowed low in her direction and said with his best French accent, "With the greatest of pleasure I will serve the beautiful mademoiselle."

Kathy giggled and he left the bedroom.

He found her slip in her open suitcase. He took it into the bedroom. The bathroom door was standing ajar. He held his hand through the opening.

Kathy took the slip out of his hand.

She said, "Thank you, D. You can come in if you like."

He said, "I'd better not. It would be too dangerous."

He was already in the other room when Kathy opened the bathroom door to finish dressing in front of him. She sighed to see the empty bedroom.

She thought of pursuing him. She knew that David would not have the will power to resist their desire. However, using that tactic to resolve their issue would be unfair. She dressed carefully and ran a brush through her short hair.

When she walked into the living room, David was over by the single window looking down at the dirty alley behind the hotel.

She said, "David, we needn't have a child. I could get a hysterectomy."

David said, "Or I could get clipped." He shook his head and said, "We both love children. We've even picked out names for them. We wouldn't be happy as a childless couple."

She said, "We might not be able to have children. You might be sterile or I might be barren."

He changed the subject. He said,

"Let's go and eat breakfast. Do you want to check out now or keep the suite for another night?"

Kathy just looked at him for a moment and then she turned away without speaking.

He pleaded, "Kathy, I want to think for a while longer."

She turned back to face him and yelled, "I thought we were going to discuss this. I thought we were going to talk."

He yelled, "We are going to talk! But I don't want to hear any rationalizations. I will believe them. I want logic!"

They glared at each other.

Suddenly they were both contrite. They wilted under each other's gaze. They dropped their heads and would not look at one another for several minutes. They stood there in silence; not even moving.

Finally, Kathy came forward and took David's hand. She said, "Let's go to breakfast, D. We'll keep the suite for one more night. We might use the double bed yet."

David gave her hand a squeeze. They left the suite together and locked it behind them. They walked down four flights of stairs and went out into the street. They found a small café a block away. After they ate, they went window shopping at the larger department stores.

Their talk was pleasant. Sometimes they were joking and laughing. At other times they discussed the political situation and various European countries. They forgot themselves as they walked in the park eating a hotdog and drinking a coke for lunch. They argued about religion again and about the existence of God. They both knew that it was a question of semantics and the acceptance of a first premise that they could never agree on. Long ago, they had abandoned the possibilities of conciliation.

It was always David who was the pessimist; the mystic and non-believer who was going into the ministry because he hoped to make a difference.

Kathy always hoped to convince him that he was wrong; that mankind should not be sold short; that there was always hope.

They forgot about the decision they must make and live by.

David persuaded Kathy to dine at one of the more expensive night clubs for their evening meal. They danced and ordered non-alcoholic beverages. That was one thing they had in common: they both came from temperance families from way back.

They left the night club at a rather late hour and walked hand in hand back to their hotel without saying a word to each other.

When they were in their suite, David tried to turn on the television and watch the late, late show. Kathy would not permit it.

She said, "We must decide this time."

They sat down together on the couch and took off their shoes. Holding hands, they shared the same settee for a footrest.

David looked at her and then kissed her. Then he said, "Be it resolved: 'Why can't we get married?'   That is the question isn't it?"

Kathy whispered, "Yes."

David said, "I'll give the biggest reason. We can't get married because we would be jeopardizing the lives of our children, if we have any."

Kathy added, "Our children would lead abnormal lives. They would not be accepted by the parents of other children in the community and would most likely be bullied at school."

David said, "We would feel guilty for loving each other so much that we gave birth to children who may be so unhappy to be alive that they would hate us."

Kathy squeezed his hand and then she said, "Our conclusion is that having children after our marriage would be inadvisable and actually a preventable cruelty."

David said, "We both want children. You wanted four: two boys and two girls; I wanted seven: four girls and three boys."

Kathy said, "We compromised on six: four girls and two boys. We've already picked out their names."

David said, "But if we marry, the kindest thing would be to have no children at all."

Kathy said, "And birth control methods are not foolproof. If I had my tubes tied or you got a vasectomy that would be foolproof. But if you died or I died, we might want to remarry and have children with another spouse."

David said, "If we marry without foolproof contraception, in a moment of weakness our behavior might lead to a pregnancy that we would not abort. We do not want to feel guilty for a misconception."

Kathy poked him in the ribs with her elbow. She said, "Don't be funny now, D, please?"

David said, "I'll rephrase that. We do not want to be guilty of procreating a child who would curse us for every living breath of his or her life."

Kathy said, "In conclusion, marriage for us is out of the question."

She didn't move for a moment. Then she began to nuzzle his neck. She kissed his cheek and ear. She whispered, "We wouldn't need to marry. I could be your mistress. You could marry someone else and have me too."

David said, "That is out of the question. If I had you, I would want no one else." He held her against him so hard that he could feel her heart beat. He said, "Marriage isn't the issue. Just loving you and having your body would make me recklessly willing to take the one in a million chance that our children could live as normal human beings."

Kathy said, "If I cared for the children and raised them away from you, your career as a Methodist pastor would not be jeopardized."

David said, "But I would want to be a real father to them. I would want to see them. I could not disown them and allow them to grow up as illegitimate. I would want to live with them in a decent neighborhood and go to a good school. I would want them to go to college, if they wanted to."

Kathy said, "We could arrange all of that and give them my last name."

David said, "The children would be curious and suspicious. Would you want your children to believe you are a whore with different fathers for each of them?"

Kathy's mouth sought David's and found it. She pressed her breasts against his chest, making sure that he was aware of her willing body.

She whispered, "Take me to bed. My period is about to start. There is no chance of conception tonight. I'm yours. I want you to sleep with me: Our first and only intercourse."

David said, "Kathy! Kathy! I love you! I want you! We will be married next Sunday evening."

His hands caressed her back. His kisses were passionate. He carried her into the bedroom and laid her on the bed.

Kathy stopped his hands from touching her body. She said, "Couldn't you take my body and then forget me?"

He looked at her with pained eyes. He fell off the bed as he knelt; as his knees hit the floor, he buried his face on the bed.

He sobbed, "Kathy! Kathy! I love you. What can I say?"

He was crying uncontrollably, his muscular frame shaking with his sobs.

Kathy sat up on the side of the bed and took his head onto her lap. She caressed his hair and hugged his head to her breasts.

Tears were streaming down her cheeks as she sobbed, "Forgive me, David. Forgive me. I knew if you had me once you would want me again and again and again. I would want you to want me. I know your sexual desire is harder than mine to control. That's why I said what I did. I love you, but it isn't right. Our children would suffer the consequences of our marriage. If I say, 'Love me tonight.' You would. Then we couldn't help but be married because we would desire each other so much. Forgive me, David." She was sobbing and her speech was all but incoherent.

David stood up and his arms went around her. He lifted her from the bed, moved her over, and lay down beside her. It was Kathy's turn to be consoled, but David could not speak. He could only hold her tight. They fell asleep and lay in each other's arms on the bed all night, kissing and hugging anytime they stirred.

It was early afternoon when they got up. David took no chances. He had Kathy dress in the bathroom with the door locked and her clothes with her. He did not want to bring her another slip.

When he went into the bathroom to shower and dress, he had Kathy in the living room in front of the television. He stepped out of the bathroom dressed in his best suit. He quickly packed all of his things and carried his suitcase and Kathy's out into the hall.

They made the last check for articles left behind together. They left the hotel after David paid the bill. They went to his old car in the parking lot and got in. David drove to the Unitarian Church where they had a 24-hour prayer chapel. Worship services were over.

In the quiet of the chapel, David

and Kathy knelt together before the altar and prayed silent prayers.

David prayed, "Pal, you've never done much for mankind, as I see it, but have compassion for your faithful servant, Kathy. She believes in you. To my darling Kathy you are brotherly love incarnate. Be for me what she believes. Be that benevolent old man of the skies and send Kathy a man, who can give her the love, and children she desires; and the respect she wants from a husband. Help Kathy find a man more worthy of her love than me. Choose the best fellow for her – I know there must be many better than I."

Kathy prayed, "Father! Father! I have never felt so miserable, so rotten. I wronged this man kneeling beside me out of selfishness. Please help him find the happiness that he deserves. There must be many women somewhere who can give David more than I could have given him. Point out these women to David! Show David the best wife he can find."

The couple joined hands now and

prayed again the same or a similar silent prayer. They finally stood up and walked out of the chapel

As they drove away now, their relationship was strained and tense.

They had not gone far toward Kathy's dormitory before she said in a voice as normal as she could manage, "Romeo and Juliet may have held a good solution to our problem."

David laughed and said, "That would be against all the principles you have preached to me these last three years. Where there's life; there's hope."

She said, "You always simplify the idea too much, but you are nearly right."

He said, "I meant that one shouldn't give up the ghost the first time life doesn't turn out the way you want. One should always hope and work for a better future. If we couldn't . . ."

David's voice caught and he stopped speaking. He swallowed the frog in his throat and said, "If we couldn't have life the way we would have liked, maybe our children could; if not our children, then maybe our grandchildren."

She thought: What children, David? We aren't going to have any children.

She didn't trust herself to speak. She let David have the last word.

When David stopped the car in front of the dormitory, Kathy asked, "Are you coming to my graduation on the twenty-second?"

He answered, "I'll come to yours at three o'clock, if you come to mine at seven o'clock."

She said, "I'll be there at the seminary at six thirty."

He said, "I'll be at the stadium at two thirty."

Kathy opened the door without waiting for David. She took her suitcase out of the backseat and climbed out of the car. A tear tried to fall out of the corner of her eye; she wouldn't let it – not now, anyway.

She said, "Goodbye, D." She was looking at his face. His face didn't have that eager, questioning look he had before the weekend.

David said, "Goodbye, K, until the twenty-second."

She slammed the door shut.

David drove away. He never once looked back by using the rearview mirror. He needed to watch the road in front of him. It seemed to be storming, but he knew the windshield wipers would not help his vision one bit.

Kathy went upstairs to her room. Her roommate was just going down for supper.

Her roommate said, "Come to supper with me, Kathy."

Kathy answered, "No thank you, Dorrie. I don't feel very hungry."

Dorrie joked, "Morning sickness?" To her surprise, Kathy burst into tears.

She sobbed, "I wish it were." Then she lay down on the bed and cried.

Dorrie came to her and tried to comfort her.

Kathy sobbed, "Go to super and leave me alone."

Dorrie left her alone.

Kathy cried for several hours then she took a sedative and went to sleep.

It was Monday afternoon and time

for Kathy's last class of the day. She took out the diagram that she copied from the blackboard during Friday's class and set it in front of her. She studied it.

Anyone who looked at the beautiful young Negro woman sitting in the fourth seat of the second row would have noticed that she had changed. Her face was dull and studious now, not bright with her enjoyment of life. Her eyes did not sparkle with her inner humor at finding so much in the world to be both serious and funny at the same time.

Kathy was not her old self. It might take several months before she would be again; on the other hand, she may always be this new hardened self.[12]

---

[12] I wrote this story in 1960 after I wrote, "Come Play with Me."

PANACEA

Owen Wingate Drysdale looked up at the skyscraper towering over him. It must have been the thousandth time he had done it that today. The majesty of those tremendous structures still did not fail to awe him.

"Jesus Christ!" he whispered to himself. "To think that they are manmade and not growing from roots that touch the center of the earth."

His eyes began to fall from the height and purity of those points stabbing the sky. He noticed first the smokestacks filling the air with foul smelling smoke. After the smokestacks would come the clothes hanging out on the fire-escapes and balconies.

Owen closed his eyes so he would not see them. He did not want to see the billboards advertising liquor and cigarettes; he did not want to see the flagpoles supporting the American flag;

and last of all, he did not want to see the litter filled street: the people, the garbage and the trash.

But, Owen opened his eyes. He needed to see where he was going. After all, he was fresh out of college and in need of a good summer job. He laughed.

"To-morrow, and to-morrow, and to-morrow, Creeps in this petty pace from day to day, To the last syllable of recorded time." He quoted softly.[13]

He saw a bench ahead. He made it his next goal. Walking toward it without looking from side to side, he could keep from looking at the faces of the other people on the street.

The bench was in bad need of a paint job. The green paint on the backside of the bench was cracked and much of it was missing. The seat and backrest of the bench had no paint at all. The gray weathered color of the wood was only broken by the dirty white of spilled popcorn caught between the boards and a scattering of brown peanut

---

[13] This is a quote from William Shakespeare's tragedy *Macbeth*.

shells and red peanut hulls. An empty paper cup was rolling back and forth on the bench; blown by the wind. The wet splotch of spilled coca-cola covered most of the boards at one end of the bench. Droplets of coke were still falling between the cracks and splashing against the filthy sidewalk.

Owen brushed aside the popcorn and peanut refuse and sat down. He watched a fat pigeon picking at someone's discarded Carmel-corn. At that moment, the earth began to shake. Owen looked up and searched for the sign of a subway entrance nearby. The trembling began to increase. There was a hushed silence all along the street. Cars stopped; there was no honking of horns.

A fissure opened in the middle of the street and spread rapidly in either direction up and down the street. There were no screams yet. No one on the street moved. Then the skyscrapers shuddered and began to quiver. A million screams echoed against the walls and into the sky. It sounded like a great cry of pain and anguish at impending doom.   People ran for basements and the open areas. A shower of debris from collapsing buildings fell upon the street. Men, women and children ran about seeking shelter.   People were trampled to death.   People were run over by vehicles driven by frantic drivers.   More people were killed by other people than by falling debris.

Owen did not move from where he sat.   He sat on the bench and watched the activity of his many relatives in the human family. The scurrying people avoided his bench, passing by on either side. Fire broke out and buildings began to blaze.   The fire followed the mutilated gas lines back until the escaping gas was burning in the street. Throughout all this, the earth continued to tremble. Finally, the skyscrapers, those man-built cedars, toppled, falling into themselves and onto the streets. Owen stayed on the bench unable to move, hardly believing what was happening before his eyes.   A wall of water moving from the direction of the lake added its roar to the sound of falling buildings. Owen watched, fascinated, as the water engulfed ruin after ruin. The tidal wave bore down upon him. Within seconds, Owen found himself enveloped by a swirling mass of water. He held his breath and allowed the wave to take him where it would. He lost his shoes. That gave him the idea of stripping himself of his clothing, which he accomplished as quickly as possible. When his lungs were about to burst with the need to expel air and inhale again, Owen fought against the current. He attempted to swim to the surface, but the water would not relinquish its hold on him. As his struggles weakened the desire to open his mouth and breathe became stronger than his will to stay alive, Owen felt himself drawn upward.

He lost consciousness.

When Owen opened his eyes, he noticed that he was lying in the bottom of a transparent sphere. He had a feeling of what it must be like within a soap bubble. Water stretched in every direction around the sphere, as far as the eye could see. Owen knew he was at the mercy of an ocean, going wherever the sea might take him – if anywhere. There was no wake about his refuge; he was floating as free as someone's lost bobber in a private lake.

Owen had surveyed his position: There was nothing he could do about it. He was so tired, so sleepy. He forced his eyes to stay open and look at the sky for a sign of sea gulls.   There was not a single bird. – The clouds looked nice. – Not even a flying fish or porpoise out there, that he could see. – Are clouds soft like pillows? – Owen closed his eyes.

It seemed that only an instant had passed before he reopened his eyes. He was looking out at the endless expanse of ocean again. He looked up. There were gulls gliding on the upper air currents. That should mean he was near land.   He turned around. He was startled. There was land: He was but a few hundred yards from its shore.

Own watched the ocean charge up the sand and recede again.   He wondered where he was. He could be anywhere. He shrugged his shoulders. It really didn't matter where he was.

The bubble lurched. It was caught up in the surf. He looked at the waves. The surf was rough; there would be tremendous undertow. The bubble lurched again, harder. It was moving. A good-sized wave had caught it right. He speeded on toward the shore in his curious craft.

Owen was studying the land that must be his new home and did not notice that the bubble was heading straight toward some rocks. He did not realize the danger his craft was in until almost too late. The transparent sphere was practically on top of the rocks when Owen noticed his predicament and quickly fell to one side. His action caused the bubble to roll, but it did not roll fast enough.

A smoothened projection on a rock struck the sphere a glancing blow. The sphere shattered. Lines marked its surface into a million shapes. The shattered bubble supported Owen for a moment before it came to pieces, spilling its passenger into the sea.

The undertow pulled at Owen at once. He tore free from its grasp and swam for the surface. A wave caught him and carried him toward shore. It died and Owen sank until his feet were touched by the undertow. He kicked his way to the surface and swam steadily toward the shore. Another wave picked him up and took him closer to the beach before it threw him down against the sandy bottom. The undertow gripped him by the waist and tried to pull him backwards. Owen's legs sank to his knees in the sand as he braced himself against the strength of the undertow. A gigantic wave crashed down upon him and popped him out of the sand like a cork out of a popgun. Owen was carried by the water to within twenty feet of escaping the perilous surf. He was brought to his knees by the undertow pulling at his feet and ankles. With the coming of the next wave, Owen ran up the beach and out of the water.

Free of the ocean, Owen turned to

look at the surf. It was a beautiful surf, a treacherous surf. Owen forced himself away from the hypnotic movement of the ocean. He entered the forest of tropical trees. A short distance from the beach, he saw a hillock covered with grass and hurried toward it. He lay down upon it, on his back.

For a moment, Owen recalled the earthquake. "So much death and destruction!" he whispered to a blade of his mattress that brushed against his mouth when he turned his head to one side. He uttered the only words he thought would be consoling. "I am the grass,[14] I cover all," he said with a catch in his voice where the middle punctuation would be. He shut his eyes tightly to help blot out the visions of people trampling other people.

Lorraine Banks made a sour face as she bit into an unripe grape. "Ugh!" she grimaced and a shiver ran down her spine. "I guess the grapes aren't ripe

---

[14] From "Grass" by Carl Sandburg, 1918.

yet!" she said to herself. It was pleasant to hear a voice, even if it were only her own; Lorraine thought aloud more often than not. It was a habit she had developed during her four days alone on this unpopulated shore.

Lorraine turned away from the grapes and walked toward the ocean she could see a short distance away. As she walked, she thought of that walk she was taking when the water came.

She had been driving her car along a country road looking at the scenery when a violent earth tremor occurred. She had stopped the car and climbed out. After the earthquake was over, she had been about to drive on when she spotted a lone flower on a nearby hillside; a flower she had never recalled seeing before. She walked up the hillside, keeping an eye on the flower.

Lorraine had been bending down to examine the odd flower and had heard a curious noise. The noise had sounded somewhat like the gurgling of a draining bathtub. Surprised, she had looked around her and saw the water coming toward her.

She stood fascinated as it rushed over her car and swallowed the hill she was on. In a moment it had pulled her off her feet. Her head slammed into a tree trunk or something, and she remembered nothing more until . . .

"Until that bubble began to roll up and back, up and back with the surf at the water's edge." She reflected aloud. "I still can't understand."

Her thoughts for the last three days had generally dealt with the significance of the wall of water, the bubble, and why she was where she was.

As Lorraine walked around the mangrove, she saw a man lying on his back.

Oh where are my clothes! She thought: I just knew I should have tried to make some.

She stepped behind a root. She peeked out from behind her hiding place.

She thought: He doesn't move!

She stepped out from behind the root.

She wondered: Is he alive?

She noticed: He has a good tan.

The man didn't move. His head was turned away from her. She noticed that he had short, kinky black hair.

She observed: He's a Negro!

She was standing above him. She couldn't see him breathing. She touched his side with her big toe.

The man sat up so suddenly that she gasped, "Oh!"

The man looked at her with wide, surprised eyes. He saw a woman with blue eyes and straight blonde hair. He noticed her figure with the critical eye of any unmarried young man.

"Venus de Milo, with arms!" he exclaimed. "Are you an angel?" he asked.

The woman laughed. "Do I have wings?" she asked.

The man was about to say, "My name is Owen Wingate Drysdale," but he didn't. He said instead, as he looked at her in puzzlement, "I am Adam."

Larraine smiled at this likeable man.

With a twinkle in her eye she said, "And I suppose that makes me Eve."

Lorraine took his hand as he stood up.[15]

---

[15] I wrote this in 1964. It got a Quiz and Quill prize in literature at Otterbein College.

MOMENT'S ILLUSION

Jimmy stood momentarily uncertain at the garage door. He was sad, so sad that he thought he shouldn't go out, but just sit on a chair and feel sad. He had a happier thought. Driving always made him happy; he would go for a drive anyway and maybe he wouldn't be sad.

He opened the garage door and walked in. The car, he remembered, needed gas. Gas was used by the internal combustion engine under the hood of the car. He had a funny idea and opened the hood of the car to look at one hundred and ten little horses he had there. He smiled at them and gave them a cube of sugar from his pocket.

Jimmy closed the hood and got into the car. His hand reached out for the key and found it left in the ignition. He backed out of the garage slowly; he wasn't in any hurry; he wasn't going anywhere, just for a drive.

He backed out so fast his little sister didn't have time to get out of the way. The six-cylinder Bellaire knocked her down and rode over her and her hopscotch game. Jimmy didn't notice.

He backed out of the driveway and onto the street and kept backing up in the left lane. He backed to the end of the block and then gunned the car forward. He was in the right lane now as he roared past his house.

He didn't notice the hysterical neighbor woman standing over his sister in the driveway.

Jimmy took the roads out of town and kept going on highway 31. He floored the gas pedal and watched the speedometer climb. The car swerved from one side of the road to the other as he watched the fat needle, a fat needle. He laughed. A fat needle.

A car honked its horn and Jimmy automatically got back into the right lane. He looked down at the speedometer again. He was going ninety. The other cars were whizzing past him, faster than telephone poles even. He looked down at the speedometer; the needle was touching the one hundred mark.

The car began to slow down. Jimmy jostled the gas pedal and nothing happened. He released it and stamped on it and nothing happened. The car rolled to a stop.

He didn't know what was wrong with the car. He didn't see that he had run out of gas. He didn't remember that was why he had gone for a drive. He had been told to get gas by the note he found on the refrigerator door, but he didn't remember.

Jimmy was going to call AAA – stalled cars were their business.

He left the car where it had stopped, half off the left side of the road. He saw a house and walked toward it. There were other houses along the road, but he walked toward that one. It had blue curtains. He liked blue as he saw it now; it was a happy color.

He passed a blue-trimmed house and knocked at the door of the house with the pretty blue curtains. He rang the doorbell and knocked again.

A young woman opened the door.

Jimmy said, "You have pretty blue curtains."

The young woman asked, "What is it you want?"

Jimmy noticed that the woman was blonde and had green eyes. He just saw her long hair with one row of curlers in it.

Jimmy stammered, "May I use your telephone. My car broke down. I want to call AAA."

"Of course," said the woman, "The telephone is over there!" She pointed towards a hallway and a hall table and the telephone on the hall table.

As Jimmy walked to the telephone, he said, "Blue is a sad color. Blue is a happy color. I like your pretty blue curtains."

The woman followed him. She was wearing a housecoat or a bathrobe.

It's hard to tell the difference, Jimmy thought. He wondered: Is she wearing anything under her robe?

He stood by the telephone table and

looked at her. She came up to the table and opened a drawer.

She said, "There's a telephone book."

Jimmy reached out and pulled on her robe belt. She was naked.

Before she could cry out, his arm went around her neck and the hand of that arm clamped over her mouth.

Both of her hands came up to fasten to his wrist.

His free hand groped between her thighs. He let her lie on the floor. The rug was soft. He felt her arms around his neck and caressing his back. He felt her exchange his kisses. The moment was wonderful.

Jimmy stood up from her. He was so drunk with pleasure and sapped strength that he fell back toward the wall. He knocked the table over when he tried to catch his balance. He settled on the floor against the wall.

After a moment, he felt so good that he went to her again. A second time he felt her arms around his neck and caressing his back. He felt her respond to his kisses. The second moment gave him such immense pleasure that he was grateful to her. He caressed her breasts and kissed her again and again. Before he stood up from her this time, he kissed her navel and rubbed his cheek against her thigh.

He walked out of the house feeling as strong as superman. He felt so good that he wanted to climb a tree.

There was a woods across the road. He began to run. A panel truck was speeding down the road. Jimmy felt so strong that he knew that he could run through the truck and cut it in half.

He ran and he hit the side of the truck and saw himself running through it and out the other side as if it were a shadow. He ran into the meadow across the road and toward the woods to climb a tree.

He never realized that he strangled the woman before he made love to her.[16]

---

[16] I wrote this to read at the Quiz and Quill breakfast in June 1967.

Postscript

Joe sat lounging in his underwear sipping a beer out of a can. His legs were sprawled wide apart on two different divans. He was fanning himself and watching television.

The apartment door opened and the ceiling light flashed on.

Joe roared, "My god, you bitch, you blinded me."

Amy didn't pay any attention to him. She set her packages on a chair, shut off the television, and then crossed the room, and opened the blinds.

She yelled, "For Christ's sake, Joe. Why do you pull the blinds on such a nice day like this? They block the flow of air. You should be outside."

She went back across the room and carried her packages into the kitchen.

Joe heaved himself to his feet and waddled after her. He said, "Damn it, Amy, can't a man watch TV when he feels like it!"

Amy set the packages on the counter. She said, "He certainly may, Joe, but not with all the blinds closed. It's just too hot today."

She went into the bathroom.

Joe called after her, "Amy, is this today's paper?"

She answered, "Yes, dear."

He grunted and began to read. Yes, he'd heard the news reports and rumors about the Champaign County high school boy, James C. Parker, who raped and murdered a preacher's wife before being run over by a truck. He'd heard all that. What was new? Oh, yes, the boy's picture was in the paper today.

Joe looked at the picture and looked at it again. He collapsed in a chair. He'd sold that boy a unit of LSD just two days before.[17]

---

[17] I wrote this after I wrote Moment's Illusion. I had a novel about the incident in mind. Same incident from the point of view of all the people involved. I probably wouldn't remember it all now.

THE MARK OF THE BEAST or
FROM THE UNKNOWN
Part one

At the beginning, it was like any other day. There was no sign or omen that said differently. In fact this day, compared with all other days, was much more beautiful and exquisite.

The sun was shining through the trees surrounding my cottage. My room was bright with light, warmth, and shining loveliness.

I awoke this day with the wonderful its-good-to-be-alive feeling. I pushed back the covers from around me and lay in bed, basking in the sun.

I cast my eyes over the walls. The rose-patterned wallpaper seemed to be glorying in the sun. Even the pictures of Christ and my betrothed, Eva, seemed alive and laughing. The flowers in the vase at the head of my bed, which the night before had been but buds, were blooming in full beauty and under the radiance of the sun seemed as if they were not roses, but marigolds.

My wondering gaze returned to Eva's picture. It was only a photograph, but it showed the beauty of her hair and face.

I could see her standing in the sun. Her golden locks glowing as if they had the radiance of fire. Her blue-green eyes shining like sapphires reflecting the dancing light. Her head was lifted towards the blue sky exposing her delicate, golden brown neck and throat. Her small round chin up tilted in the proud, pleased manner so becoming of her. She began to smile, her cheeks reddening and forming dimples. Her nose even gave her additional beauty. These and her lovely figure made her a creature of charming grace and the most exquisite of God's creations: a beautiful woman.

I shut my eyes and began to dream of how wonderful it will be to have her as my wife. With a feeling of happiness and satisfaction, I arose from bed and walked to the open window. Drawing back the curtains more, enabled the sun to cast its rays into the darkest corners of my room.

With my view less obscured, I could see all the way across the field and up the distant hill. The morning glories shone as diminutive ivory flowers scattered at random across the pasture and along the fence. Even the cattle seemed to be raising their heads to catch every ray of sunlight available.

As I stood in awe of this wonderful day, I began to note a change. The morning glories began to wither and close. The sky darkened and the gentle breeze that was blowing diminished.

Puzzled, I turned my gaze to the sky, expecting to see dark clouds. My eyes opened in astonishment. There were no clouds. The sun wasn't there as usual. It had nearly disappeared and was barely a dot in the sky.

Utterly bewildered, I sat heavily down on the edge of my bed. I was dazed. Was I seeing things? Was I dreaming? After a few moments of unease, I again turned toward the window and stared out anxiously.

Now the cattle seemed aware of the radical change in their surroundings. They were mooing and milling about scraping their hooves against the sod.

The bull was the first to head for the fence and the open road. His flight brought all the other cattle running after him. They hit the fence with the impact of a ten ton truck moving at one hundred miles an hour. Splinters and posts flew everywhere. Many of the lead cattle were caught in the wire and trampled by other cattle stampeding over them.

Seeing the gravity of the situation, I quickly dressed and ran outside. The cattle were headed across the field on the other side of the road.

I raced toward the barn and threw open the door. The car was in the first stall. I ran to it and attempted to get in. It was locked. The keys – I had forgotten the keys.

My heart beating faster and faster, I darted back to the house. I looked but I could not find my keys.

Where are they? What did I do with them?

I told myself to calm down; that everything will be all right.

I began to shake all over. I went to the sofa and threw myself down. After what seemed a century, I was calm enough to think.

Now, what did I do with my keys?

Ah ha! I put them in the top drawer of my dresser last night.

I sighed and went into my room.

Once I was outside again, I noticed that it was much darker than before. Not wishing to spend too much time trying to understand the works of God, I got into the car and started it. It usually needs to warm up a while before it can move.

After waiting a minute, the car was ready to go. I pulled out of the barn, down the lane, and out to the road. I got to the spot where the cattle broke through; I looked over the extent of the damage. It wasn't much, but it would be expensive.

I glanced across the road where the

cattle broke through again. I noted the additional damage and turned the car through the gap in the fence and started across the field.

The field seemed infinitely long, but soon I came to the other side. The fence here was damaged as well. The cattle were still running at a good speed. I went through the wreckage and started across the stream on the other side of the fence.

There were cattle lying on the bank, trampled and bleeding. Even their flesh could not be salvaged; they had been gashed that much. The remainder of the cattle had gone on across the stream and up the bank on the other side.

I had a strong desire to go on but some of the cattle were in pain and needed to be destroyed. I turned the car around and went back home.

I put the car away and got out the small truck. I stopped the truck in front of the house and went inside. My guns were still in the gun cabinet where I put them last fall. I brought out my Winchester and looked for shells. Luckily

I wasn't out.

Taking several boxes, I left the house and got back into the truck. I lay the rifle on the floor and the boxes of shells on the seat beside me. I started the engine. After a moment of idling, I drove down the lane and out onto the road. I stopped at the first break and, finding some injured cattle still alive, I put them away. At the break on the other side of the road, I destroyed the dying cattle there as well.

After crossing the field, I came to the stream. There I found eleven head still alive and badly injured. Surprisingly, there were no injured cattle at the break in the fence above the stream. Any injured cattle had been dragged down the bank by the stampede.

When all the injured cattle had been destroyed, I crossed the stream and drove the truck along the newly made cattle trail. Their hooves had cut into the sod forming a strip about thirty feet wide. It was getting darker. I switched on the lights to enable me to see tree stumps and other obstacles in the trail.

After a few minutes, I noticed by the headlights some curious looking mounds in the trail ahead. When I was close enough to see clearly, I recognized my cattle. I got out of the truck, taking my gun with me.

I went cautiously toward the nearest carcass. The cow was brutally mangled. One leg was missing and much of its flesh was scattered at random around it. The animal was stiff as though it had been dead for a day and not just an hour or so. I quickly went from one mound to another. They were all dead, mangled and torn in the same fashion as the first.

I was puzzled. None of the cattle had been trampled as all the others had been that I killed on the way to this spot. What could have slaughtered a herd of cattle that quickly?

I looked up at the sky. There was not a cloud or star in the sky. The moon wasn't out. It was only eight o'clock in the morning and it was as dark as dusk. The only visible light was coming from a pinhole of light in the sky that was once that glorious sun I had seen that morning in my bedroom. I went back to the truck and got my flashlight out of the glove compartment.

After investigating the whole surrounding area, I did not find a sign of more cattle or any other animal. I knew that if a marauding predator had done this, I would have seen some sign of it. There was no animal that could jump from one prey to another and kill a whole herd of cattle in that way without leaving some footprints or other sign; at least no predator that I knew about.

It had not darkened this much until I got here. If some unknown predator had been nearby, I think I would have seen it. I could not have missed it if it had escaped in my direction. It could have escaped in a different direction, but I had gone all around the area where my herd of cattle had been killed and I saw no tracks at all.

How could an animal kill all of my cattle and then jump fifty feet or more away? I had searched an area that large around my mangled herd and I saw no tracks within fifty feet of the herd. I didn't even see cattle tracks leaving the area; coming into the area, but not leaving it.

That left only one possibility: A cow went berserk and killed all the other cows and then committed suicide. Just the thought of that was just absurd.

I began to feel nauseated. I decided to leave before the bloody sight overcame my senses.

I walked falteringly to the truck and got in. I leaned my head over the steering wheel and almost upchucked, but I was able to keep it down.

I knew that all the dead cattle needed to be buried. That would be a major undertaking. I would need help, besides; it was too dark to do it now. The unusual darkness was also of great concern.

I wondered what my friends would say about all of this. I needed advice. I started the truck and went back the way I came. Once I reached the road, I drove toward town.

Brier City was only five mile from my farm. It was a town with a population of forty-nine. I knew everyone in town and they knew me. Most of the people in the community surrounding the town were farmers. The town itself had a grocer, a plumber, and a mayor. The mayor served as our minister, mortician, sheriff and postman. There also was a school teacher, my Eva, and a few other townsfolk.

As I was driving I tried to remember all the things that I wanted to tell about the happenings of the day. I soon got to the city limits.

Within the limits, I began to slow down. Then I heard a splintering of glass and a splat. Adam Thomas's elephant gun bellowed in the dark. I dove for the floor and hit the brake with my knee. I applied the brake so hard that the engine died.

I yelled, "Hey! Quit shooting! It's me!"

Adam knew my voice.

In the distance came a gruff, "Adam, what in the hell are you doing? Didn't you recognize Keith's pickup?"

I recognized the voice of Deacon

Jones. He was the minister, sheriff, mortician, and postman. We all called him Deacon, most of the time.

A reply came from a voice that was quaking slightly, "Ah, Deacon, I thought he was the monster." It was Adam's voice.

Deacon said to Adam, "Well, at least you didn't do him in." Then he yelled, "Come on out, Keith. It won't happen again!"

I thought, "I hope not." I stumbled out of the cab and walked over slowly. I was feeling a little unsteady on my feet and uncertain about Adam.

Adam's voice quavered a little as he said, "I'm awful sorry, Keith."

I said, 'That's all right, Adam. I may have done the same thing after what's happened at my place."

Adam held out his hand and I shook it. Then I shook Deacon's hand.

With the making up out of the way, Deacon said, "You mean you lost cattle too?"

I answered, "I sure did. Oddest thing happened. Beautiful day; all of a sudden, it turns like this and the cattle stampeded."

Adam asked, "Did all of your cattle get slaughtered like mine?"

I said, "They sure did, Adam; But slaughtered isn't the word for it. They were mauled and body parts scattered everywhere."

Deacon said, "I just came from his place. His cattle are a mess even for a butcher. I don't think they can be salvaged for any meat."

I asked, "Adam did your cattle stampede?"

He said, "A little, but not a whole lot. I heard them running, but by the time I got outside they were all dead. It happened that fast. And I didn't hear any bellowing. How could something kill them that quietly? So I came to town and got the sheriff."

Deacon, the sheriff, nodded his head in agreement.

I said, "Well, you know those two fields across from my pasture."

They both nodded and said, "Yeah."

I continued, "My bull led the cattle

on a stampede. They broke through the fence, went across the road, broke down that fence and stampeded all the way across that field, through the far fence and over the stream. I found dying cattle at every fence and in the stream. I found what was left about a mile from the stream. Every cow mauled to death in a very gruesome way."

Deacon said, "You aren't the only ones with trouble. Bill Johnson, Clyde Holloway, and a few others had the same thing happen to their cattle."

I asked, "Did anything happen here in town?"

Deacon said, "Yes."

I asked, "What happened?"

He answered, "We didn't have a church service this morning."

It was then that I noticed that Deacon was dressed in his Sunday best. I hadn't thought about church.

I asked, "Why not?"

Deacon answered, "I was working on my sermon when Adam came and wanted me to be a witness to something he said that I would not believe. I went with him as Sheriff and didn't have time to change. After I saw it, I believed it. By the time we got back, others were here with similar stories."

Deacon and Adam turned and walked toward the store. They looked back when they saw that I wasn't coming with them. They stopped walking.

In answer to their puzzled faces, I said, "I have to get my rifle."

They both gave grunts of understanding and again headed toward the store.

After listening to the many tales of grief that were told in the store, I began to lose interest. No one knew the cause of all the happenings.

Another bored person blurted out, "Quite an enigma, ain't it."

A second person exclaimed, "A what?"

The first person said, "An enigma, you know, a riddle, a puzzle." The speaker saw a frown on the faces of several people in the store. He added,

"Aw, what's the use."

A silence ensued.

I looked from one man to the next and then over to the women and children that were clumped together for fellowship and safety.

The silence was broken by a piercing scream and then a moan. I lifted my rifle into position and faced the door. Others faced the door with their own guns. A few men even ventured out the door, but they came scrambling back, bowling each other over on their way back inside.

One of them said, "I saw it! I saw it! It's all bloody! It's a giant!"

The baleful moans and screams began again.

Very much puzzled, I ran to the door and went out. There I saw it too, a bleeding hulk of bone and flesh. It happened to be what was left of Sam Jenkins, a bachelor who owned the farm north of mine.

I knelt down beside him and placed my hand where I thought his chest to be. I felt no pulse. Then I realized that

I had placed my hand on his hip. As mangled and torn as Sam's body was, I prayed that he was dead. He was. I sighed in relief and thanked God.

I carried his body inside and set it on the floor so everyone could see that Sam was not the monster. Sam had no relatives so many in the store wanted to throw his body back out into the street.

Deacon and I, and a few others wanted to give him a decent burial. We put it to a vote. The decision was to bury him and the sooner the better, considering the condition of the body.

Deacon took a new blanket off of a shelf and wrapped the body in it. A couple of others found wood to make a coffin. Nails and hammer from supplies in the store were used to build it.

Deacon sent out word that there would be a funeral at the church in about an hour. The whole community was invited to attend.

As one of the pallbearers, I helped carry the coffin to the church. Everyone in the store followed us over. Most people thought that the church would be the safest place from danger; and if they were to die, let it be in church.

We carried the coffin into the church and set it on a table at the front of the center aisle. That way everyone could walk by and touch it and pray for Sam's soul, if they wished. For obvious reasons, it would not be an open casket.

I was thinking that I should get Eva and bring her to the funeral. I wanted to see her anyway. I was worried about her with all that had happened.

I headed up the aisle to walk down the street to her house. Many more people were coming into the church from outside. As I got to the front door, Eva came in with some of her neighbors. I hugged her but we did not kiss. Public display of affection was frowned upon in our conservative community.

I took her hand and we walked to the front of the church and took seats in the second pew. We whispered about all that had happened on the farms and in town. Then she whispered, "I love you."

And I whispered back, "I love you too."

She leaned her head against my shoulder and we held hands during the service. That was about all that was allowed in public.

The service was short. Everyone filed by the coffin and touched it and said goodbye to a neighbor and friend.

When it came time for the burial, Deacon went back to the store for shovels. The rest of the men gathered around the coffin to decide who would dig and who would mourn.

Our discussion was broken by a scream of pain. Many of us quickly ran outside. There on the ground in front of the church was Deacon. His body was convulsing and blood was pouring out of his mouth and his torn chest. His eyes were glazed and staring.

Clyde Holloway bent over Deacon to see if he were alive. Clyde yelled and pulled back from Deacon. His wife screamed and ran forward. Clyde turned toward us and we could see that his chest was torn open with a gaping hole. His wife put her arms around him to hold him up. Then she stood up and let his body fall to the ground. She fell backwards and we could see the gaping hole in her chest dripping with blood.

Everyone ran back into the church in a panic.

The remaining men drew lots to see who would go out and stand guard. I got the job.

I turned toward Eva. She had fear in her eyes also. I took her hands in mine and looked into her eyes. I grinned. She smiled. I dropped her hands and took up my rifle and went outside.

I could see the bodies of Deacon and of Clyde and his wife. I tried not to look at them. I bravely sat down with my back to the door of the church and held my rifle, at ready, on my knees.

I stared out into the blackness and thought about the sunshine of this morning. I shivered. My thoughts were little comfort.

Inside, without my knowledge, Adam Thomas was telling others that we were facing pure evil and the only way to satisfy pure evil was with a sacrifice.

The death of Jesus on the cross wasn't enough. More had to be done. Our ancestors knew what to do. This kind of evil required a human sacrifice of a member of the community. After that, their prayers and requests would be granted by the gods that our pagan forefathers worshipped for thousands of years before Christ.

This idea met with the approval of most of the community in the church. They were so frightened. They were willing to believe anything and try anything to be spared what had happened to Deacon and the Holloways.

Someone asked Adam, "What kind of sacrifice is the best?"

He said, "You all know. It is the sacrifice of a beautiful virgin; that always satisfies the gods. And maybe it will satisfy the pure evil that we are facing outside."

This was met with the approval of the majority. Those present looked from one to another, but there was only one among them that qualified.

Eva understood from the way their

eyes fastened on her that she was to be the sacrifice. She began to back away from their stares. They began to close in on her. Panic seized her. She opened her mouth to call out to me, to scream for help.

A hand closed over her mouth choking back her screams for help. Someone tore at her dress. She kicked; she bit; she scratched and struck out with her fists. Someone hit her on the side of the head.

When she regained consciousness, she tried to move and couldn't. Her hands and feet were tied to something that pinned her down on top of the altar; and she was naked. She looked around. The whole community was gathered around the altar. The men, the women and the children were watching with rapt attention. Some of them had their mouths open and they were drooling. All of them were breathing deeply with their excitement.

Then Adam Thomas came toward her from the group surrounding her. He had a chef's knife held with both hands.

He raised it up above her chest.

Eva screamed in fear and horror.

I was whistling and peering into the darkness. I was watching for whatever it was that was killing cows and people.

I heard Eva scream. I knew her voice. I had teased her with spiders or worms often enough to know her scream.

I scrambled to my feet to go into the church. It was locked. I drew back and rammed my shoulder against the door. The lock broke and the door swung open.

Adam had pumped his knife-filled hands three times above Eva's chest or I would never have seen the blade plunge into her chest. He drove it in with such force that it went through her body and I heard a thunk as the knife bit into the wood of the altar.

A chill ran up and down my spine. I didn't think of using my rifle. I dropped the rifle. I wanted to kill him with my bare hands.

As I ran forward, people tried to

stop me. I knocked them down; I bowled them over; I trampled on them. I got to the altar and put my hands around Adam's neck. I was choking the life out of him.

Then his chest burst open exposing his heart. I pulled my hands away from his throat and stood back.

Right before my eyes, his heart burst open. I was sickened by the sight of his blood flowing out of his chest and down the front of his pants.

I wondered if anyone would blame me for his death. I looked around me. No one was advancing on me. On the contrary, they were backing away from me and the scene of their human sacrifice. To my surprise and horror, they were yelling and screaming in abject fear, pain, and agony. All about them, one by one the chests of men, women, and children burst open. In one instance it looked as though the victim was turned inside out, with his skin on the inside and all of his blood vessels and organs on the outside.

Whatever or whoever was killing

these people, it was doing it to a rhythm. Every other second a new victim would scream in pain as his chest burst open and he died.

People stopped running and began to watch it happen, knowing it was only a matter of a very short time and it would happen to them.

I backed away from the spectacle before me. I backed to the wall and found myself leaning against the huge cross mounted to the wall behind the altar. I watched from there.

Excruciating death came to them all, one after another, until I alone was left.

I began to sweat. My breathing became heavier and more frequent. I was next. It was inevitable.

I wondered.

Should I go to the altar and die with Eva?

Should I try to escape?

I looked over at Eva. Adam had fallen to the floor after he died.

Eva died instantly. Her eyes were wide with fear and the scream of terror was frozen on her. She may not have felt much pain or it could have been excruciating.

I went to her and put my hands on her face. I pulled down on her cheek muscles as I held her face in my hands. Then I moved her mouth closed and pressed my lips to her lips in a kiss.

Finally I closed her eyes. I stood back. Now Eva looked as though she were asleep.

I wondered why I wasn't dead yet. I had counted. The rhythm of the killings had been steady. I should be dead. Maybe it wanted to play a game.

I looked around. I looked for the nearest exit. The windows; maybe I could get out of a window.

I went around Adam and moved to the wall left of the huge cross. I put my back to the wall. I felt something touch me. It was cold. I couldn't see it. I moved immediately to my right.

Keeping my back against the wall, I scooted rapidly along it. The feeling of being touched left me. For a moment I felt safe; secure.

I was jarred to a stop. I had hit the

corner of the church sanctuary. My hands moved along the adjacent wall. There was no door nearby. Now I moved along the new wall to my right. I had gone only a foot and I ran into the cold. I moved back to the corner. I turned the corner to go back the way I came. I bumped into the cold to my left. I moved back into the corner. I was trapped. I braced myself with my shoulders and arms against the two walls.

When I felt the cold touch again, I kicked out. I kicked hard. I kept kicking. I felt the cold chill of the invisible monster grab an ankle then it grabbed the other ankle.

I kept kicking but the cold moved up my legs until they were frozen in place with my knees against the two walls that made the corner. Then I felt the cold moving up my thighs and into my groin.

In more ways than one, I was frozen in position.

The cold moved into my pelvis; then into my stomach; then it was in my throat.

I was the last one alive.   It was playing with me.

I couldn't move.   It could kill me anytime it wanted. I waited. I couldn't talk; my tongue and larynx were frozen.

The cold moved into my brain.

I stopped feeling anything at all.[18]

---

[18] I wrote this in 1960. I started in Biology class and wrote until I got to this point. It was probably the only time I didn't say a word in class all day. I was a sophomore at Mississinawa Valley High School in Darke County, Ohio.

THE MARK OF THE BEAST or
FROM THE UNKNOWN
Part two

At first, all was silent. Then I began to hear my own smooth breathing: In and out; In and out.

Soon I heard foot steps and voices.

A masculine voice said, "Don't worry, Miss Barker. He will be alright."

Then I heard, "Oh, doctor, how can I be sure? He was so sick I thought he would die?"

I recognized that voice immediately. It was Eva's. I was elated. She was not dead. I let out a long sigh.

I heard a startled, "Doctor!"

I soon felt a competent hand checking my pulse.

The male voice I heard earlier said, "He's alright. He is awake and listening to us."

There came a happy sigh of relief from Eva. Then she said, "After finding him in that condition Sunday morning, I thought he would never live."

The doctor's voice said, "Never underestimate the powers of healing." He paused a moment and then asked, "By the way, how did you happen to find him? You know if you had been an hour later, we would never have gotten his appendix out in time."

Eva's answer came in those soft bell-like tones that I so loved, "Keith and I had planned to go to church together and picnic afterwards. When Keith didn't pick me up at the house, I guessed that he had car trouble or slept late. I decided to wait for him and I got a book to read and sat out on the porch in the sun. After awhile, I got worried and called him at the farm. When he didn't answer, I got my car out of the garage and drove to the farm. I honked, thinking he may have had an emergency with an animal somewhere, but he didn't come out to greet me. I went into the barn and hunted for him. When I didn't find him there, I went into his house and called out. He didn't answer so I went looking for him in the living room, the dining room and the kitchen. Finally I went into his bedroom and I found him. He was so feverish. I tried to move him, but he was too heavy for me. So I called the grocer, Allen Shoemaker, to bring his station wagon out there. He came and between us we got Keith to the hospital."

The doctor said, "It was lucky for him that you came along when you did. He would be dead now if you hadn't found him."

There was more conversation after that but I did not listen. I longed to open my eyes, but I was afraid that all I would see would be darkness. I hated darkness.

After some wrestling with my fears, I finally put them aside and opened my eyes. And there was light! Glorious light!

The sun was shining through a window. I smiled and thanked God.

I looked about me. I was in bed; a hospital bed. On a sheet was printed:

Boulder City Memorial Hospital.

Boulder City! That was over fifty miles from home. What was I doing here? Oh, yes, I remembered, it had to do with my appendix.

It doesn't fit: This hospital; my appendix; the other. My scrambled thoughts were interrupted.

Eva said, "He's awake." She was smiling brightly. Then I saw a man dressed in white: My doctor?

The man said gently, "Looks like he's feeling pretty good."

Eva was soon at my bedside smothering me with kisses. I was rather bewildered, but happy. I showed my mood by putting my arms around Eva and pulling her close to me.

Then I felt a sharp pain in my right side. I placed my hands there and ground my teeth in agony.

Eva noticed my face and put her hands on each side of my pillow. The man dressed in white helped her gently to her feet. Then he examined me.

After pulling the sheet back over me, he said, "Just too much strain on the stitches. He'll be alright if he lies still."

Eva came to me again and kissed me on the cheek. She whispered, "Bye, bye."

During my stay at the hospital, I awoke many times in the night. The first few times, I screamed when I saw the darkness. Then I would get hysterical and hyperventilate.

After the first two times, they gave me a sedative. I didn't like the sedative. It made me feel like I was dying again. I didn't like to lose consciousness in the dark.

They began to give me the sedative right after Eva left me each afternoon. School was in session and she came to see me after work and stayed about half an hour every day. I would sleep until the sun was up. That seemed to work for me.

Eva found out about this routine and confronted me. It was Saturday morning and I was to be released on Sunday afternoon. She closed the door to my room and I told her all about my dream, if it was a dream.

After I was finished, she said, "Oh you poor dear. I think it's about time we were married."

I said, "How can I ask you to marry me when I can't sleep without a sedative?"

She said, "You are not asking me. I am asking you."

Then she left me.

When she came back, Deacon Jones was with her. She had our marriage certificate and we were married by Deacon Jones. The doctor and one of the nurses were our witnesses.

She stayed overnight with me in my hospital bed. She wasn't a virgin, but I didn't mind. That fact made part of my nightmare a lie.

How could Adam Thomas sacrifice her on the altar as a virgin, if she wasn't a virgin?

The next day after breakfast, she took me home. I had been in the hospital two weeks to the day. The neighbors had been taking care of the livestock.

We had sex in the morning and sex in the afternoon when she got home from work. Then I took a sedative and hoped I would sleep all night.

During the day, Eva taught school and I did the farm work. We used condoms when we had sex. I did not want to have a child when I was afraid of the dark.

When summer came and school was out, Eva told me that it was time for me to wean myself off of the sedatives. We went to bed together just before dark. We had sex and then I went to sleep.

Eva was there when I woke up in the dark. She held me when I woke up screaming. She held me and calmed me down. She would go with me to the bathroom. We would take turns. Then we would go back to bed and have sex again and I would fall asleep with her in my arms.

After a month, I could sleep through the night. If I awakened in the dark, I would feel Eva beside me and go back to sleep.

It was late August. Eva would be going back to work after Labor Day. I was beginning to worry that I would have to go back on sedatives during the winter with its short days.

One night, I woke up in the night and I didn't fear the dark. Instead, I thought, "I wonder what the stars look like tonight."

I moved carefully away from Eva. When I wasn't touching her, I moved out of the bed without squeaking the springs. I tucked Eva in so that the sheet was tight about her. I got into my clothes and then I crept out of the bedroom and went outside.

It was a very clear night. The stars were brilliant. I could see many constellations and three planets: Jupiter, Venus, and Mars. The moon was not in sight. It was very dark.

I began to tremble. I felt the cold touch my feet. I said to myself, "No. Please no. Help me God. Help me."

I looked up at the stars again and searched for the Big Dipper and the North Star. When I found the North

Star, it calmed me.   I relaxed and just looked at it. After a while, I lay down in the grass and looked up at the sky.

Hours later, Eva sat bolt upright in bed.   I wasn't with her.   A great fear gripped her heart.

She called out, "Keith? Keith?"

When I didn't answer, she began to tremble.   She turned on the light at the night stand and got out of bed.

She dressed quickly in jeans and shirt.   She didn't bother with panties or bra.   She pulled on her boots and headed into the kitchen.   She looked all through the house, calling, "Keith? Keith?"   She was frantic, but she called softly.   If I was sleepwalking she did not want to startle me and send me into a panic attack.

Finally she went out the backdoor and there she saw me lying on my back in the yard.   I was spread out on the grass with my arms and legs wide-apart.

She thought that I might have killed myself.   Once I had considered it when I had awakened with that terror of the evil killer gripping my soul.

She rushed to me and lay on top of me. She kept saying, "Keith! Keith!" as she put her arms around me.

I had fallen asleep in the yard. When I felt her arms around me and heard her calling my name. I woke up and hugged her and kissed her.

We were on fire with desire. I opened her shirt and pulled off her pants. Then I took off my clothes and put them down on the ground for a bed. We made love in our backyard without a condom.

Afterwards we lay there looking up at the night sky until the sun came out and dawn spread its beautiful colors across the sky.

Our daughter was born nine months later. We named her: Dawn.[19]

---

[19] Part two is a sequel I wrote the weekend after I wrote Part one. I was never sure how I should end part one. Should I end it with everyone dead? Was I an experiment and aliens had killed everyone but me? What do you think?

SECOND EARTH

First came the Sun, then Mercury, and Earth – no moon, but an Earth encircled by an asteroid belt two hundred thousand miles above the equator. After Earth came Mars and its two moons, the fragments of the lost planet, Jupiter and its ten major moons, Saturn, Uranus, and Pluto. Pluto? – No Pluto.[20] No ring around Saturn, but there was Titan!

Captain Andrew O'Connell of the Nine Planets' Space Exploration Team calibrated the distances between the planets and the sun he saw before him. The distances were approximately the same as he remembered they should be for his home solar system. He leaned back in his seat and scratched his head.

He said aloud, "I wish the General had sent another man along with me on this excursion. I could use a little coordinated advice! . . . Well, for a

---

[20] This was written long before Pluto was eliminated as a planet.

closer look at the third from the sun."

O'Connell centered the third planet on the view screen. He increased magnification slowly so as to discover if he had the same sensation as coming toward home. He saw first what appeared to be the twin American continents and then portions of what may be Africa and Europe. He gasped with wonder as he zeroed in on the northern continent and saw a scene that brought nostalgia for Earth and the United States of America to his mind.

"God!" he exclaimed. "It doesn't seem possible that two systems could be so much alike. This could be home!" he mused as the absurdity of that thought struck him, "The Moon could be claimed to have exploded, the Rings of Saturn to have been absorbed by Saturn's atmosphere, and Pluto to have been thrown out of orbit and lost to the solar system. All the differences in planetary characteristics could be claimed to be due to evolutionary changes."

He looked again at the North America before him. There were roads and cities.   In the area that could contain the United States, O'Connell saw only five metropolises.   There was a city near the southern end of Lake Michigan; one where St. Louis would be; one at the top of Chesapeake Bay; one where Seattle would be; and the last one near what would be the location of Galveston, Texas.

O'Connell continued to photograph, take measurements, and compile data as the planet spun on its axis. When the northern continent came into view again, O'Connell pulled the switch and radioed the data to Earth; then he went to eat and get some sleep.

After twenty hours of sleep, O'Connell returned to the control room and set a course to intercept the third planet on his ship's course around the sun. He periodically checked his progress during the next ten days and finally took over the controls himself when he was within a thousand miles of the asteroid belt. He skirted what he assumed was once a moon and went into orbit five thousand miles above the planet's surface.

After five more days of extensive studies during which he twice took his ship into the planet's atmosphere to test it, O'Connell finally prepared for a landing. The city that O'Connell had named St. Louis seemed to be the largest, so he decided to ground there.

O'Connell maneuvered his craft until he was in an orbit a few miles outside the planet's atmosphere. Then turning the tail of his ship around to face the direction he was orbiting, he gave instantaneous thrust to equalize his orbiting speed. In the grasp of gravity, the ship began to drop toward the planet's surface.

As O'Connell maneuvered his ship over the city, he saw a large area that served as a spaceport. He flew his ship over the port and found a spot big enough for his ship to ground near a building he took to be a terminal. When he came near the chosen spot, he flew vertically until his tail was directly above the spot. By decreasing thrust by the right amount, he dropped to the surface and grounded gently.

When O'Connell climbed out of his airlock and stepped to the ground, he was met by a tall, blonde-bearded man. His greeter wore boots, tights and trunks. The clothing accentuated the man's splendid physique.

The blonde smiled and spoke in a language that O'Connell could not understand. However, the man held out his hand as though for a handshake.

O'Connell understood the traditional Terran symbol of friendship and, taking the man's offered hand, he said, "How do you do."

"Ah!" said the blonde man, much pleased, "You speak English!" He looked closely at O'Connell and asked, "You are not one of our own come back after so long, are you?"

O/Connell answered, "No, I am not."

The man said, "Oh, forgive me. I am forgetting my manners. My name is Thor Odin, and on behalf of the Supreme Council, I welcome you to Earth."

Despite half-expecting to be greeted with such words, O'Connell's mouth dropped open and he nearly collapsed from the shock passing through his brain. A moment later, he was the composed diplomatic-poker player that he was paid to be.

"Well, Odin," O'Connell said, "I'm Captain Andrew O'Connell." Then he added good-naturedly, "I'm not sure that 'Take me to your leader!' is really appropriate in this instance."

Odin laughed and his blue eyes twinkled with his humor as he said, "That classic request has quite a history. And even though you had not voiced that thought, you would have eventually been taken before the Supreme Council. We have been expecting you since we observed your craft approaching us sixty-three days ago. I apologize if the welcoming committee does not fit your customs or expectations, but very few people were interested in your possible arrival. If you came, they could see you on the view screens or talk with you in person – if they wished."

O'Connell said, "I notice that the other craft at this port is of a design far advanced from my own." He turned toward Odin, waiting for him to explain how a lost colony of far Earth could have attained such great strides in science.

Odin said, "Your ship went out of production two hundred years ago. We now actually have little need for this craft here." Odin gestured to indicate all the ships at the port then he continued, "We developed a much better mode of transportation one hundred years ago."

O'Connell asked, "Then why do you keep so many?"

Odin answered, "We keep developing these because we may one day need to defend ourselves from an enemy. Also, many of our people use them for recreation." Odin stopped talking and looked at O'Connell and said, "My but you have much to catch up on."

O'Connell did not bat an eye, but his throat constricted a moment as he absorbed this second gentle thrust at his sanity. Odin's remark did not ruffle O'Connell's outward composure. The Captain began to form a list of questions in his mind.

Before O'Connell could ask one of his questions, Odin said, "Follow me." Then he led the way to the terminal.

The terminal's huge lounge was completely deserted. O'Connell and his guide walked the whole length and went through a doorway into an adjacent office room. A dark-skinned woman with glossy black hair was standing at a filing cabinet. She turned toward the two men.

O'Connell saw the face and sinuous figure of a beautiful woman. She wore a long-sleeved one-piece garment that resembled a swimming-suit and calf-high scarlet boots to match.

O'Connell's breath caught in his throat as he watched her open her mouth to speak to Odin.

"Uh, Fay," Odin began, speaking very pointedly in English, "this is Captain Andrew O'Connell." Odin looked at O'Connell and asked, "Andrew?"

O'Connell nodded.

Odin then said, "Andrew, it is my pleasure to introduce you to Miss Fay Tyra."

"How do you do," the man and the woman said at the same time.

Before any conversation could develop, Odin asked, "Is the Chief in?"

Fay pushed a curled lock of her long hair away from her face. She said, "Yes, but he's busy. Would you please be seated?" Then she looked at O'Connell and gave him a special smile only for him.

O'Connell sat down and feasted his eyes upon a creature of the kind he had been denied for six years.

Odin remained standing, but moved to the large window at the other end of the room and stood looking out.

Fay was aware of the wolf-eyes watching her as she worked. She finally blushed and turned to face O'Connell. She saw in his eyes the admiration and lust he had for her.

O'Connell stood up and said to her, "Please sit down." And he motioned to the chair that he just vacated.

Fay sat down and O'Connell pulled up another chair and sat down facing her.

Fay smiled at him and said, "I saw your ship ground through the window. It's a very old model, but the antiques usually have much more ornate designs. Is that ship the oldest model in your collection?"

O'Connell gave her a long and puzzled look and said, "My ship was issued new to me six years ago."

She exclaimed, "Oh! No wonder it looks in such good condition."

He asked, "Are all women on this planet as beautiful as you?"

Fay smiled and faint color rose to her cheeks. She said, "Most women of Earth are more beautiful than I. Terra is a land of beautiful women and handsome men. Just ask Mr. Odin."

O'Connell shook his head and said, "That first, I will not believe. Not even an orchid could be more beautiful than you."

Fay blushed and asked, "Were all of our ancient explorers as able to compliment a woman?"

He frowned and said, "But I am not one of your ancient explorers!"

Fay looked at him curiously and said, "Oh, but you must be! We are the only people in the universe that ever spoke English." She laughed and added, "And we are the only ones who ever built spacecraft of the type of your ship."

O'Connell shook his head and said, "This is all wrong."

She asked, "Are you not of Earth?" There was a sound of wonder and surprise in her voice.

He said, "Why of course I am from Earth, but . . ."

She interrupted and said simply, "Well, this is Earth – Terra!"

O'Connell laughed and stood up. He placed his hand on her forehead and said, "Either you are sick, or I am."

Her forehead was cool; O'Connell used the back of his hand to push her long black hair away from her face. He swallowed trying to release the tightness in his throat. His hand moved to the back of her neck and he bent his head and kissed her lips.

Fay made no response, only continued to sit very still.

O'Connell stood up and took his hand away.

The woman only looked into his eyes. No look of revulsion or censure was on her face.

A man poked his head out of the doorway and said, "Mr. Odin, will you please bring our guest in."

Odin crossed the room and went through the doorway expecting O'Connell to follow him uninvited.

Before O'Connell followed, he looked into the woman's bright blue eyes. He asked, "Will they," he was referring to the men in the other room, "allow me to see you again"

She answered, "Yes, if you wish."

He was disappointed with her response and asked, "Have you no thoughts?"

She said, "Yes, I would like that very much."

O'Connell gave her a grateful smile and entered the other room.

Odin sat in a chair to the right of the desk. The man behind the desk was rather heavy set. The latter indicated that O'Connell sit down in the chair in front of the desk.

The man behind the desk smiled kindly at O'Connell. He was the perfect father image. He said, "I understand that your name is Andrew O'Connell. I am the present Chief of the Supreme Council." He bowed his grayed head and said, "Philip Tyra, at your service."

He smiled, his eyes sparkling, and continued, "You undoubtedly met my daughter, Mr. O'Connell." He hesitated for just a moment. Then he said, "It is good that another one of you has made it back. You'll find many changes. The Earth you knew suffered a terrible Atomic War. Very little of its political and social structure still exists. We, who rebuilt, established order from chaos and tried, for history's sake, to put the pieces in their former places. But some pieces were missing. We are still rebuilding. So much for your briefing! Now for those things that would be of interest you."

"Mr. Odin," the chief asked, turning

to his subordinate, "how many years of back pay is coming to this man?"

Odin answered, "I would guess three hundred years, at least sir; maybe more."

The chief turned back to O'Connell and asked, "What was your rank at the time you left Earth?"

O'Connell laughed and said, "You gentlemen have the wrong man. It may be that I look like the man you want and our names are similar, but my full name is Andrew Johnson O'Connell. You may have sent out an Andrew O'Connell, but not one with that middle name. That should prove I don't come from this planet!"

The Chief smiled and said, "Actually, Mr. O'Connell, we have no assurances at all that you are one of our earlier explorers. But, that ship of yours is of the type we sent out on trips three hundred years ago. There are only," the Chief picked up a paper on his desk and looked at it, "one hundred and fifty-four ships of that type presently registered in our worlds. All these ships belong to the explorers and the descendants of the explorers who brought them in; and your ship is not one that is registered."

O'Connell laughed again and said, "Then that proves I am not of this world!"

The Chief shook his head and said, "Mr. O'Connell, on the contrary! It proves you are one of our earlier explorers, because the records – names of men, serial numbers of ships, ranks and any pictures taken – were somehow destroyed during the last three hundred years; probably a result of the war. We have no record of how many actual explorers there were, or how many ships there were, but we assume that the ship's design is a good means of identifying our men. . . . Now, what was your rank before you left?"

O'Connell pleaded, "But I tell you that I do not come from here!"

The Chief looked sadly at Odin and then he smiled and said gently to O'Connell, "Nevertheless, Mr. O'Connell, could you please tell us what your rank was when you left."

O'Connell said, "I am Captain of the Nine Planets' Space Exploration Team."

Odin said, "Captain, that entitles you to accumulated back pay of $2000.00 per month, tax free."[21]

The news gave O'Connell no happiness.

The Chief said, "Captain O'Connell, we must insist that you have a complete physical and psychological examination. I will have Miss Tyra show you to the doctor."

He pressed a button.

A feminine voice asked, "Yes, Chief?"

The Chief said, "Miss Tyra, will you show Captain O'Connell to Dr. Mason's office?"

"Yes, sir," came the reply.

A moment later, Fay entered the office and called, "Captain O'Connell, please come with me."

O'Connell stood up, shook hands with the Chief and Odin, and walked out of the room.

---

[21] This is 1964. In today's dollars that is approximately $16,000.00/month.

When the door was closed, the Chief sighed and looked at Odin. He said, "Thor, it is a pity. Captain O'Connell must have been a very bright young man when he was sent out. So long a time and by himself! I hope his mind is not too affected."

Odin nodded in agreement. Then the two men laughed at a private joke.

As they walked along, Fay looked curiously at O'Connell. She said, "You are so young to be a captain."

O'Connell smiled at her and asked, "What part of Earth is this?"

She answered, "The Grecian Sector."

He said, "Oh?"

She said, "Yes." Then she asked, "Have you ever seen the Acropolis?"

He lied, "No."

She said, "We could visit it tonight after you have been cleared by Dr. Mason."

He said, "You seem to have no doubts at all that I will be cleared."

She wondered, "Should there be

some doubt?"

They stopped in front of a closed door.

Fay said, "This is Dr. Mason's office.

He said, "Thank you."

Fay turned to leave but O'Connell caught her by an arm. He asked, "Fay, may I kiss you again?"

Fay was about to refuse his request, but she looked into his eyes and saw his fear and his lack of self-assurance. She understood his need for belief in himself and for someone to trust; she gently took his head in her hands and pulled it down and kissed him with her mouth open.

O'Connell responded to her kiss with only his lips; his arms hung limp at his sides.

He said, "Thank you."

She said nothing as she watched him enter Mason's office before she returned to work.

The air-car came to a halt in the parking lot. Fay stepped out before

O'Connell had time to walk around the car to help her.

"There!" she said and motioned with her hand, "the Acropolis!"

O'Connell turned to see and his eyes grew wide in wonder – it was the whole building: Complete to the hill and the steps; just as it must have looked to the ancient Greeks.

Fay was so earnest about her pleasure in showing him this acropolis that he didn't laugh aloud. He laughed inwardly to himself as he thought of this Acropolis towering above him.

It wasn't anywhere near Athens. It was on a hill of the central plains of North America! He remembered, though, that the Balkan Peninsula of this world did not resemble the one that he knew at all; there was much less of it. There was no Greece.

Fay said, "Come," and taking his arm, she led the way to the steps.

As they climbed the steps, she asked, "What did Dr. Mason say about you?"

He answered, "Dr. Mason said that I

am physically sound, but suffered a gradual mental deterioration due to such a long time alone. I am to be off duty indefinitely." As a second thought, he asked, "My ship won't be disturbed, will it?"

The woman shook her head and said, "No. Your ship is yours and no one may enter it until you give them permission and sign a waiver of your rights to its contents."

She saw O'Connell release a great sigh of relief.

The couple sat down on the steps before Athena.

Fay asked, "Tell me. What was it like three hundred years ago? History says that there has been much change, but you saw it with your own eyes. Wasn't it very much like it is now?"

O'Connell frowned into the darkness. He asked, "Will you believe me when I say that I am not from this planet?"

She said simply, "Yes. Then what was it like on your home planet."

"We have three billion people living

on Earth. We once had more than twice that amount, but many have left to colonize the other planets and solar systems within our reach. There are nearly five million ships of the type like mine that explore and chart the galaxy."

He was about to tell her more, but she interrupted and asked, "But what was the social structure like"

He said, "The social structure is not at all like yours. We have classes due mostly to income, but also, in part to education. There is widespread discrimination that affects everyone. But mostly it is Caucasian discrimination against the colored races. You can see that a classed society and discrimination would inhibit the intellectual growth of all living in such an environment."

She asked, "Did you have an organization to enforce laws?"

He answered, "Yes, we have a police force, for we have crime. You have one psychologist or psychiatrist for every twenty citizens – a much greater ratio than that of our police officers to our citizens. You have no laws but something you call your 'moral traditions.' We punish those who break our laws; you give those who disregard your 'moral traditions' a psychological examination and only hospitalize them if they abuse their rights and the rights of other citizens."

He was remembering some of the discussions during his debriefing with Dr. Mason.

She changed the subject when she whispered, "Don't you think it's a beautiful night?"

He said, "Yes, it's lovely, although I do miss the Moon."

She whispered, "A moon? We had one once upon a time. Of course, your planet had one."

He said, "Yes, it had one. But it's not exactly a moon. It's more nearly a companion planet because of its huge size."

Fay said, "Our people sang a song called, 'Shine on, Shine on, Harvest moon' a long time ago. It's an old, old folksong."

O'Connell swallowed the air that had

caught in his throat and looked closely at the woman. Fay began to hum the tune she had mentioned and shortly, O'Connell was softly singing the words.

Fay exclaimed, "You know the song!"

"Yes." Said O'Connell meekly, stricken with a terrible thought: Am I from this planet?

O'Connell recalled an earlier conversation with Dr. Mason.

Mason said, "Captain O'Connell, you mean to tell me that your planet is behind that Red Giant over there in the sky?"

O'Connell answered, "Yes, sir."

The doctor said, "But our earlier explorers have never reported the existence of a solar system such as you have just described."

O'Connell insisted, "Sir, the system I come from is hidden behind that large star, this red giant!"

Dr. Mason said, "I already told you that our explorers have been beyond that star and have not found a Sol-type sun with nine planets in that location."

The doctor stopped talking and shook his head in regret; then he said, "Go out and have a nice evening. You need a long rest."

So he went to supper with Fay. He enjoyed her company so much. Now they were at the Acropolis. He wondered what their plans were for him.

Fay asked, "A penny for your thoughts?"

O'Connell smiled at her.

She whispered, "I'm rather chilled."

O'Connell put his arm around her waist and drew her to him.

She turned her head and nibbled at his ear with her lips. Then her arms went around him and her lips found his mouth.

O'Connell's hands shook nervously before he began to caress her back. Finally, he crushed her to him

It was the woman that broke the spell or he might have gone all the way with her at the feet of Athena.

As he was kissing her throat, she whispered in his ear, "I have an apartment and I live alone."

She felt him grow tense, and then slowly relax to pull her to him again. He kissed her once more on the mouth and then he released her.

He liked this girl; he had been about to go all the way with her; and then she spoke; and he remembered where he was.

O'Connell said, "I'm not sure that I should do that."

She whispered, "But I want you." And she pressed her cheek against his cheek.

O'Connell hesitated. He frowned as he thought. Then he said, "All right. Let's go."

They walked down the many steps holding hands. They got into the air-car and Fay drove swiftly.

All the while she drove, she felt the eyes of the man on her every movement. By the time they reached her apartment house, she was flushed and a bit embarrassed.

As her hand reached out to cut off the power and remove the key, O'Connell's hand closed over her hand.

She turned toward him with open mouth and eyes that were soft with their understanding. She was ready for him.

But her eyes grew wide and puzzled when she saw his face. O'Connell's brow was furrowed and his eyes were hard and cold.

He hurt her hand as he forced her to let loose of the key. He took her purse and threw it out of the open dome above them. His hands moved over her whole body removing all buttons and the contents of her pockets.

Fay was too frightened to resist.

O'Connell picked her up and set her down on the other side of him. Then he slid under the stick and drove at top speed to the space port. He drove up before his own ship and opened the air-car door.

Fay pleaded, "Andrew! Don't leave!"

O'Connell hesitated.

Fay reached out and put her arms around him. Tears were streaming down her face.

O'Connell took her in his arms and kissed her tenderly on the tip of her nose. Then he hugged her tight.

He said, "You make a perfectly loveable secret agent. I'm sorry."

He released her and took her face in his hands. He kissed her lips gently.

A moment later, he turned his back on her and ran to his ship.

Fay was still gazing up in the direction of the star behind which was O'Connell's destination, when she felt a hand on her shoulder.

The Chief asked, "Couldn't get him to stay?"

Fay said, "I'm sorry, Chief. I liked him too much to make him believe this was his Earth."

The Chief smiled down at her. He began to smooth her hair with his hand. He said, "My little daughter, I hope he left you your heart."

Fay broke into sobs, her shoulders shaking as she cried.

The Chief opened the air-car door,

pulled her out, and put his arms around her.

He soothed, "It's all right, Honey. It was our fault. We have no one to blame but ourselves."

The Chief sighed and his sadness was visible on his face. He said, "You and he – the interaction of your personalities was the unknown factor. We thought we had taken every precaution, but we were beaten by what we considered a nominal unknown."

Fay lifted her head from the Chief's broad chest and looked into his eyes.

She asked, "Father? Why was it necessary?"

"Fay," he said with his thoughts as painful as a migraine headache, "we didn't want him to know! We didn't want him to find out." His voice trailed off at the end.

He held his daughter tighter in his arms while the unpleasantness of his thoughts reached their peak. Then he relaxed and released her.

They stood together, father and daughter, looking up at the faint point of light they both knew to be a deadly red giant.

Philip Tyra had his right arm around his little girl. He took a deep breath. He motioned with his left hand, outward toward the stars.

He said, "He's out there somewhere, headed to nowhere. He's wondering why he left! He's wondering whether he should come back . . . but he won't. He'll keep on going until he's beyond the red giant; he'll keep on going, looking for his home."

"Will Andrew come back?" Fay asked, breaking the old man's train of thought.

The Chief smiled and bent to kiss her forehead. He said, "Sweetheart, when he arrives at that point in space where his Earth should be and finds only empty space, it will be quite a blow to his organized mind. He may fall back on what we told him, but I doubt it. He will think of a hundred possible reasons for his Earth's absence from where he thinks it should be."

Philip Tyra, Chief of the Supreme

Council of their Earth, said to his only child, "Yes, Andrew will come back. After he has confronted the most formidable of his many possible conclusions, he will ask, 'Why should a planet and its people be destroyed and its history stolen?' Then he will ask, 'Why should one man live and a whole world die?' That question will haunt him until it is answered."

The Chief concluded, "He will be back; and I will have the answers waiting; and you, my own little Fay, may have the one thing to console him for his loss of identity, your love."[22]

---

[22] I wrote this in the spring of 1964.

Dear Reader,

LIGHT AND TENDER BLUE and Other Stories from the Sixties is a collection of fourteen short stories or novelettes written between 1960 and 1964. One or more can be labeled: Science fiction, Fantasy, Horror, Romance, Race Relations, or Satire. They were written while the author was in high school and college in the sixties. They have never been published before. They are in the order for the best read. However, you can read them in any order that you choose. I hope you will enjoy reading them.

In 2013, I began to e-publish. I wrote **Summer** in 1998, but I published it first because it is dedicated to my wife, Carolyn, the love of my life. It is about pain and suffering and the difficult choices people face, and how love can overcome anything. It is a book for adult readers.

When the Dew Fell on the Okra is my first children's book to be published. It was written in December 1966. When I graduated from Otterbein College in January 1967, I gave it to people who had been a help to me. Thanks to Rebecca Swift, my illustrator, it is now available for you to give to someone you care about.

Before My Shotgun Wedding is a book for all ages. It is about two best friends growing up in the mountains of Kentucky and going to college before an abusive father with a shotgun forces them to get married.

The sequel, **After My Shotgun Wedding** is for adult readers.

I have eight more novels available for adult readers: **Foundling, Clarence or Claire, Katya and the Solar Wind,** two sequels to **Katya: Triangulation** and **Shoreen; Qarka Girls, Symbiosis, And Angels Feared to Tread** are the most recent science fiction novels to be published.

First Eighty-five Poems was my first volume of poetry. All poems were written between January 1, 1959 and August 1, 1963.

Second Hundred and Sixty-three Poems was my second volume of poetry. All poems were written between August 1963 and March 1967.

Third Hundred and Sixty-eight Poems is my third volume of poetry. These poems were written between March 1967 and March 1981.

Fourth Hundred and Nine Poems is my fourth volume of poetry. They were written between April 7, 1981 and February 23, 2002.

Fifth Volume of Poetry: Falling in Love is my fifth volume of poetry. These poems were written between July 1977 and October 1981.

Sixth Volume of Poetry: Falling in Love Again is my sixth volume of poetry. These poems were written between October 15, 1980 and December 13, 1981.

Seventh Volume of Poetry: Cultivating Love is my seventh volume of poetry. These poems were written between February 1982 and March 1985.

I try to give you a hint of all the feelings I had as I matured as a person. Every one of us has to struggle to be good and kind and loving.

I have loved many girls and women in my life. And a part of me still loves them all. I wish you a lifetime of loving and caring for others and being loved and cared for.

If you are a struggling Christian and have difficulties sorting out your priorities, I had the same kind of problems in my youth. I hope you find my poems meaningful to you. And I suggest that you write your own poetry. Rappers aren't the only people who can express themselves. Everyone can.

As a pastor and theologian, I do not separate the sacred and the profane. The difference is in the human mind and not in life itself, just as evil is in the human mind and comes out of the choices people make and not from the devil who made me do it. The devil has nothing to do with it. We are the ones who choose to do evil or good. The whole world is in our hands.

Enjoy the books.

Paul David Robinson

Paul David Robinson, BA, MDiv, Pastor, Retired

https://www.amazon.com/author/pauldavidrobinson

https://www.pauldavidrobinson.com